GW00871561

Guess Who W

by Bernar

Author: Bernard James Luckhurst
© Bernard James Luckhurst

Printed By Blissetts of London

ISBN: 978-1-905912-70-4
A catalogue record or this book is available from the British Library.

First published in the United Kingdom in 2020
By Bernard James Luckhurst

To Lyn

with thanks fo. you.
friendship and many
kindnesses over the years

Benard

1

For my dear wife, Madaline,
without whose love,
support and encouragement
this project would not have endured.

Foreword

This book is a collection of fifty totally fictitious and sometimes satirical conversations from the back of my London taxicab. In creating these discussions I have drawn largely, but not totally, from the invaluable information produced by Wikipedia on a whole range of persons and subjects. Other references, too many to mention, have also been accessed along with personal knowledge and experiences. I am extremely grateful for all sources and pay tribute to those who have shared their knowledge of information and events to the benefit of others.

These conversations were created primarily for my grandchildren who might wish for a very brief insight into some of those persons who have had a role to play in our world over the years. Nowhere in each narrative do I disclose the passenger but there are numerous facts included in each story that give clues as to their identity and some subtle hints that have a bearing on the story but it is for you to determine just who it is. In the majority of cases that will be quite easy but should you become baffled or seek confirmation, the 'fare' is disclosed, in reverse spelling at the end of each story.

My forty years of service as a London police officer provided a concrete basis for the additional fourteen years that I spent driving a cab around the Capital. This combined fifty-four years dealing with the public of our great city has convinced me that the majority of people are decent and honest and well balanced in their outlook on life. There are exceptions, of course, but life would not be the rich tapestry that it is without those who, for good reason or bad, stand out in our memories.

Individuality and idiosyncrasies are valuable to our way of life if only, at times, to remind us that it takes all sorts to create the whole and we are richer for the presence of those who do not quite match our expectations. I shall always be pleased to see the multi-coloured Mohican haircut or the ghostly presence of a 'Goth' or even the pristine appearance of the City worker to assure me that freedom to live in London as we wish without hurt to others is something that we should cherish and always protect.

Please enjoy the challenge of identifying the subject and if something in the brief synopsis provided should whet your appetite then take the opportunity to broaden your mind and read wider and further.

Bernard James Luckhurst
May, 2020.

Guess Who Was in My Cab Today

1

I was driving my cab in Ambrosden Avenue alongside Westminster Cathedral today when a man in a caftan hailed me.   He was about 30 years old in a heavy flowing robe with a shawl over his head.   He had a long beard and piercing blue eyes; the eyes of a leader.

"Hello Sir, where can I take you?" I asked.

"I need to go over to Chiswick, towards Kew Gardens," he said.

On the way I offered him an opportunity to speak and said, "A lovely day, do you have any plans?"

"Yes" he replied, I am meeting some friends this evening for a meal but I have had a bad morning.   I was with some banking associates and they tried to beat me down on a business arrangement which made me very, very angry so much so that I threw them out of my hotel room.

He was clearly annoyed at this experience so I just said that we all have difficult days and tried to change the subject.

He then said, "Earlier I was in Victoria Street and I felt sorry for a homeless man so I bought him a sandwich, then before I knew what was happening several more men came around so I went off and bought a whole load more but obviously too many for when they had finished there were about twelve sandwiches, mainly tuna, left over."

Not wishing him to become too down I asked about his planned meal with his friends in the evening.

He said, "I have booked a room upstairs in a pub in the Chiswick High Road for twelve or thirteen guys but I am not looking forward to it at all because one of them has been speaking badly about me and I intend to challenge him about his behaviour which will cause some trouble.   He added somewhat lightly that he would like to go for a walk in Kew Gardens afterwards and would only need to be attacked by a group of yobs to finish off a really bad day!

At this moment he signalled for me to pull over near a building site just past Dukes Avenue. I stopped near a skip that had some rubbish burning and as he got out a gust of wind blew some heavy smoke into the cab and he disappeared. My first thought was that he had bilked me but suddenly a hand came through the smoke with a £50 note. "Keep the change" he said and was gone.

I called out "That's very kind of you, Sir" and as an afterthought shouted after him "God bless you". A deep voice from high up replied, "And you my son."

I looked up and saw high on the scaffolding a labourer with a mischievous grin on his face.

The Arab's face was familiar but I couldn't think why.

hterazanfosusej

Guess Who Was in My Cab Today

2

I had just dropped off a fare near the Royal Hospital, Chelsea when a lady Chelsea Pensioner in her resplendent pillar box red uniform asked me to take her to St. Martin's Place at the north side of Trafalgar Square. A few seconds of thought for the best route and I instinctively headed off towards the Pimlico Road.

I was ready for a chat so asked, "Somewhere nice to go today?" as an opening conversation piece.

"Yes" she replied, "I'm going to meet up with some of my old nursing patients. I used to be a nurse in Belgium at the National School of Nursing."

"That's very interesting" I said "and now a Chelsea Pensioner. Do you come from Belgium?"

"No", she said, "in fact I come from Norfolk where my father was a Church of England clergyman." She then went on to tell me that there was a military hospital in Brussels where there were a large number of English soldier patients and although she trained in London she knew Brussels so was very happy to accept a post there as matron. She said that she had been made an honorary member of the Royal Hospital Chelsea because of her work in Belgium.

I prompted her to tell me some of her stories but she just said that whilst it was very rewarding to nurse fellow Englishmen (and some French) she was frequently frustrated by the lack of care and facilities that prevented her from helping these soldiers as much as she would have liked. She said that often in the evenings after treating their wounds she would assist these poor ill men to compose letters home and whilst she could not always get hold of the medicines that they needed she could help them in other ways.

Often, she would be writing into the night by the light of an oil lamp because the normal lighting had gone down. It was very hard she said when she could not help their pain or properly tend their wounds. On rare occasions she had managed to repatriate them but had to be very careful not to upset the military command.

I told her that it must have been tremendously rewarding when she did succeed but she said not everyone was happy. Many did not want her around to see how these poor souls were treated or how supplies were in such demand and often half hinted that she was probably a spy making up stories. Several times they told her that she should leave and go somewhere else but she resisted telling the command that she was going nowhere as long as the patients needed her. At one point someone actually said that if she didn't go 'something might happen to her that would not be very pleasant'!

With that we arrived in St. Martin's Lane and she indicated to set her down near the statue at the junction with William IV Street. She paid her fare and as she got out there were two very loud bangs that came from a passing old motor cycle and with that she was gone.

I thought what a truly wonderful lady and one so dedicated to her chosen vocation that despite the threats to her personal safety she would never abandon those left in her charge.

llevachtide

Guess Who Was in My Cab Today

3

I often like to drive down the Strand for it is usually not too busy and the bus lane does help a lot if the traffic is a little heavy.

I had just turned from Trafalgar Square (or to be more precise from St. Martin's Lane) into Duncannon Street and was passing the side entrance of the South African Embassy when I was hailed by a rather portly man dressed in dark suit with a homburg hat and golden watch chain across his waistcoat. He was also carrying a sleek walking stick with which he waved to catch my attention.

"Yes Sir" I said as I pulled to a halt, "where can I take you?" "To Parliament Square please" he roared more than said. Thinking that this is not much of a fare and is certainly within walking distance I pointed out that traffic was a little heavier around the Strand and in Whitehall but not wanting to appear unwilling to take him I apologised for the congestion and set off on the journey.

"I would normally walk it especially as I am not in a hurry but the gout is painful today" he volunteered. I drove straight across from Duncannon Street into the forecourt of Charing Cross Station to turn round and joined the queue at the south end of the Strand waiting to cross the Square and head into Whitehall.

"Lovely day" I said giving my passenger a chance to talk if he wished. "Yes", he said, "I love London and when you walk you see so much more AND you don't know who you might bump into. However, my foot is playing up so much today I thought that I would take a comfortable ride."

He then went on to tell me that he used to be a war correspondent abroad but was now home to pursue a political career. In fact he had just had lunch at the South African Embassy with some old newspaper colleagues and was off to catch up on the political scene.

"Do you favour any particular political party?" I asked. "Well," he said "I was in with the Tories but they became so concerned with feathering their own nest that I left and joined the Liberals. Then there was some trouble abroad and the Libs who were in power were gullible enough to think that they could deal with this foreign upstart and believed everything that he told them. They caught a cold over that so I left and came back to the Tories."

"So what now?" I teasingly asked. 'Prime Minister in waiting?"

"No, I don't think so." He answered, "Most of my political colleagues don't take me seriously and laugh at my warnings on the international scene but I have confidence in my own judgement and try and caution them to little avail. It probably has something to do with my mother being American. She always told me, 'tell the truth, son, no matter how much it hurts, it will always pay in the long run'. The British don't like the Yanks; you know what they say about them; 'over-paid; over-sexed and over-here.'"

He went on, "I believe that you must always give the people something to look forward to. Set your goals and keep going; speak out whenever you have the chance and give the people hope. For me it is; 'Forward, unflinching, unswerving. Indomitable, till the whole task is done and the whole world is safe and clean".

"In the meantime keep busy, I do, I am just finishing my sixth volume on the last War - thanks cabbie," he said interrupting himself, " just drop me here by the gates – opposite that statue. Have a nice day."

llihcruhcnotsniw

Guess Who Was in My Cab Today

4

Like most cabbies whenever I approach the pedestrian crossing in the Abbey Road I look over towards the recording studios to see which celebrity is leaving and who might need a cab. This morning was no different but there was no one on the doorstep so I carried on only to be shouted at by all four of a motley crew of youths just up from the crossing.

My first thought was why do I need four boisterous young men in my cab, especially four dressed as they were. I suppose my generation would describe them as bohemian, certainly their dress was not conventional. Most of them had very long hair, they were all skinny, no beards (although one had a clipped moustache) and an assortment of clothing that would have been more acceptable on a clown rather than someone in St. John's Wood. Skin-tight jeans or colourful trousers was the clear dress code. One had on a loose-fitting singlet showing his upper body hair and, unbelievably, a crown on his head! Two of them were carrying guitars.

Ah well! A fare is a fare so I pulled over. "Yes guys," I asked. "We want to go to Wembley" they almost sang in chorus. "Wembley Stadium?" I offered. "No, the Arena" they said together as they clambered in.

Was the best route going to be the Harrow Road or the Western Avenue? I decided on the former and off we went. There was so much noise coming from the back of the cab that I could barely think. They were laughing and shouting and one of the guys was playing his guitar in an almost mesmerising way quite oblivious of the others. He was surprisingly good.

They then all started singing about riding a bicycle then they went on about breaking free – I'm not sure where from but it wasn't my type of music. This variation of songs was continuous and the one with the crown on was clearly the lead man for did most of the solo singing.

At several points I had to call them to kill the volume especially when we were in traffic where lots of other car drivers were looking at us. I didn't want a passing police car to pull us over and berate us for our noise. They were quite good about the chastisement but soon reverted back to the music. There was a little break from the loud noise when the guitar man started playing "God Save the Queen' and the rest kept quiet . I thought it was a bit odd for them to respect the National Anthem and I almost expected them all to stand up. Anyway they were enjoying themselves and not really a great problem to anyone else.

This tribute over they soon got back to their raucous sound and then they were all singing "We will rock you" over and over again. They were in tune but it did go on and on.

As we approached Wembley Stadium they seamlessly moved from "We will rock you" into a very loud and enthusiastic "We are the Champions." I could almost feel the sea of football supporters surging down Olympic Way *en route* to pay homage to their respective teams.

As I turned towards the Arena I couldn't stop myself from joining-in with my four passengers and at the top of my voice I also was singing "We are the champions" just about the only song among their repertoire that I recognised (apart from the National Anthem).

On leaving the cab the one with the crown, for some bizarre reason, asked if I was from Turkey.   Puzzled, I replied to the negative and he explained, "its just that you remind me of a friend of ours called Tolga Kashif.'

Very strange but one of the more interesting fares that I have had.

puorgpopneeuq

Guess Who Was in My Cab Today

5

I was heading back into town along the Du Cane Road in Shepherds Bush when a tall black man hailed me near the Wormwood Scrubs Prison. He was a good 6ft, well built and, I would guess, about 60 – 65 years old. His hair was grey and closely cropped but he had a gentle face and a ready smile.

"Hello Sir" I greeted him, "Where to?' He very politely said, "The Supreme Court in Parliament Square please." He had a little trouble bending down to get in, probably back problems I thought. Once settled I headed off towards the Western Avenue mentally planning my route.

"Have you had a good day?" he asked in a raspy, gravelly voice that had a twang that I couldn't first place. "Yes, thank you" I said, "although I'm always cautious of picking up a fare near a prison in case I inadvertently aid an escaped prisoner. You haven't just climbed over that wall have you?" I joked.

He laughed in a kind of staccato way that immediately reminded me of Frank Bruno in his boxing days –'Hello Harry, Heh Heh Heh'; Know what I mean Harry, Heh Heh Heh.'

"Not today" he said, "but I've spent many years in such a place in my youth." "Really?" I said thinking that this man sounds quite interesting, "All behind you now though is it?" "Yes" Heh Heh Heh, they thought that they had beaten me Heh Heh Heh but I won in the end. Heh Heh Heh"

I thought that if he wanted to tell me more he would say so but best not be too forward in quizzing him, he seemed a little vulnerable and I thought his face and grey hair indicated a harsh early life.

Anyway, my role as a cabbie is not to pry but just be willing to listen if someone wants to off load. Its actually amazing how many people want to tell you, a stranger, their life story in quite intimate details.

Perhaps that is what it is, you are a stranger and they will never see you again so it's safe to be open.

After a short period of quiet he said, "I used to be quite a problem in my younger days. Some didn't like me because I tended to be outspoken and said what I thought; others claimed that I wasn't open enough and should have condemned more but in my country then there was always someone who would quickly denounce you to the authorities and then you were in trouble so you had to tread a fine line. That's how I finished up in prison."

"But surely" I said, "if you stick by your principles – and I'm not trying to dig into your personal life – then at least you have right on your side."

"Heh Heh Heh" he chuckled, " Can you imagine as a black man ever trying to explain your *principles* as you put it, to an authority that has always had the upper hand and the intention to keep you down?" "No, I'm lucky to have got out when I did and when things did change I still had my life intact but many of my friends did not. My desire to see poverty eradicated and healthcare for all was once a dream and it will take a long time to achieve this but that is now for others. I wanted what you have, freedom under the law. Remember, my friend, a winner is a dreamer who never gives up. Heh Heh Heh."

On arrival at the Supreme Court he quickly paid his fare (plus a tip) and sauntered off not into the Court, which I expected, but to a nearby statue where he sat down on the base and opened up a sandwich wrapped in foil, a rather meagre lunch for such a noble man, I thought.

alednamnoslen

Guess Who Was in My Cab Today

6

Doughty Street is a rather quiet road in Clerkenwell that runs parallel to the Grays Inn Road. Meandering down this delightful oasis of well kept, late 18thC houses, I was hailed by and elderly gentleman sporting a moustache and long goatee beard.

"I need to go to Fleet Street to see my publisher for 3 pm" he volunteered. Looking at my watch I saw that we had half an hour to make the journey. "No problem" I said and manoeuvred a 'U' Turn.

En routé he was reading The Times and said, "You know, I do enjoy reading these articles by Thomas Stuttaford. He is a doctor and has a way of making the most boring of subjects interesting and I look forward every week to his column . Have you ever read them?"

I confessed that I had not. "However", I said, "I do admire people who have the gift of writing well.   Now you said that you were off to see your publisher does that mean that you are an author?"

"Hardly and author" he replied, "more a writer than an author." "Is there a difference?" I asked. "Well" he replied, "I tend to write on sociological issues; I like to observe people and situations and speculate why a particular scenario has come about.   I am more about the true circumstance of everyday events and situations rather than a fictional story where everything is pure imagination."

"But surely" I prompted, "even novelists draw on their real life experiences to make up the story." "Ah!" he responded, "but novelists are doing just that, they are writing a story and can weave a web that cannot be fully supported, indeed, need not to be supported by true life events.   They are merely using that experience as a basis from which to launch their tome which, I would suggest, is more for popular consumption rather than the true sociological writer who is presenting a purist reflection of life."

"It is interesting though what you say and I could, perhaps, deviate occasionally into the more lucrative side of publishing and even let my writing run wild for I could then incorporate some of those immensely fascinating people that I have come across in life."

He seemed then to be letting his mind wander, "Yes" he said to himself rather than me "that Bob Fagin who I used to work with in the factory when I was young was a memorable character and I could work something around him, I suppose. And all those leeches of lawyers that almost ruined my father – I could get my own back there as well and portray them for what they are rather than the pillars of society that they think they are"

I called him out of his reminiscences as we turned into Fleet Street, "Where would you like, Sir?" I asked. "Oh! Here will do nicely thank you." He replied, "Keep the change" and off he walked.

I then saw that he had given me an old, out of circulation, £10 note.

snekcidselrahc

Guess Who Was in My Cab Today

7

There is such a proliferation of Fitness Centres all around London that, despite the high membership fees, I find it hard to understand how they can all make a profit.   But, I suppose those who do go and regularly torture themselves must believe that it is doing some good to their physical and mental wellbeing.   I must admit that I have yet to see any of them come out with a smile on their face.

Earlier today I was passing one such establishment in the Earls Court area when a very attractive young lady who had just left the gym flagged me down.   She looked extremely fit but somewhat flushed and clearly upset.   My first thoughts were that if self-flagellation does this for you then it is not for me.

She jumped in and asked that I take her to the Middlesex Hospital in Mortimer Street where she said that she had an appointment.   As I headed off she just dissolved into tears, sobbing and beating her fists on her thighs.

I never like to see anyone upset and mindful that sometimes it helps to unburden oneself I gingerly asked if she would like to talk.   "It's that husband of mine" she said, "we have had difficulties in our marriage and now we are getting divorced and I fear that it will not be very amicable.   He has another woman and I now must go my own way.   My two boys are the most important thing in my life now and that is all I care about.   Some time ago I was abroad and when I returned I just couldn't wait to hug my sons again after being away from them.   It's not as if I see them everyday.   They are both at boarding school so I only have the holidays with them."

"I guess that it is now up to me as to how I live my life. I will go out to dinner with whomsoever I wish and I will mix with whomsoever I wish."

"I will try to do some charitable work to make good use of my time. I have formally associated myself to several charities to help as best I can and it is no worry for me if I shake hands with an AIDS patient, like the ones that I will be shall meeting later, they really need to be able to relate to someone who is not going to condemn them for their illnesses. HIV does not make people dangerous you know."

"I will go to The Passage to help care for the homeless and the down-and-out. I will continue to send flowers to little girls who are dying of cancer and write to those unfortunate women in refuges who are frightened out of the lives of their former partners. Someone must show that they care and if my presence gives them that comfort then my time is well spent. Nothing brings me more happiness than trying to help the most vulnerable people in society, I just wish that I could do something more for them."

As we turned into the Mortimer Street I said, "Well, I can only salute what you are doing for the unfortunates of this life, I am sure that those individuals recognise your care and for them, perhaps, what you are doing is more than enough. Certainly, to have received a visit from the mother of our future king is something that they will not quickly forget. Perhaps now it is you who need a break somewhere to be able to reflect on your life and maybe come up with a way forward."

"Yes" she said, "that is just what I am going to do. I have a trip already planned. I am going to Paris with a dear friend for a few days and we shall stay in the Ritz. I will do some shopping and we will probably go out to dinner in the evenings. My friend has arranged for a local chauffeur and someone to look after us so I guess that we will be quite safe. I shall certainly not be bothered by my husband whilst there."

When I stopped the cab she bounded out a lot happier than when she got in. "Thank you cabbie, " she said, "You have been very kind in listening to me, please keep the change." With that she strode off having given me a generous tip on top of the fare.

selawfossecnirpanaid

Guess Who Was in My Cab Today

8

The four of them sat in my cab chatting away whilst I drove them from a non-descript building just off of the one-way system of King Street at Hammersmith to another non-descript building on the Albert Embankment.

Three older men, each around 60 plus years of age, and a younger very smart and well-dressed lady in her mid to late forties were animatedly discussing something.

By the way they were talking it was clear that it was she who was in charge for whilst they each held their own in the conversation they deferred to her when she sought to make a point. They were all joining in on the general conversation and discussing something that had apparently happened a long time ago. As a matter of good manners I never intentionally listen in on passenger's conversations but it is inevitable that, at times, you will hear what they are saying without really understanding what they are talking about.

Such was the case here.   It appeared that they had been instructed to enquire into some incident from the past for the lady made it clear to the others that despite their views they were going to spend some time looking through old documents and then going to interview people and challenge them on what they had said some years ago about something or other.

One of the men, a south-London boy if my identification of his accent was correct, was adamant that it was a complete waste of everyone's time and they could be better employed elsewhere.   The second man who seemed more cerebral in his thinking was trying to make the point that at the time of this incident in 1984 (I think they said) this particular person or that was engaged in an activity which took him out of the equation. He seemed to have an encyclopaedic grasp of dates and places that he could quote off of the top of his head.

The third man didn't get as excited as the other two but when he interposed with a point they seemed to listen to him and followed his train of thought almost out of deference to his older years.

The lady appeared quite exasperated at times and kept saying something about times had changed and they couldn't just go off and behave as they had in the past.   She was more conscious of what might happen if they didn't 'follow the rules' and was insistent that they act properly in looking into this incident for it was she who would have to convince those who were instructing her and answer any criticisms.

The south-London boy kept making the point that unless they were allowed to 'properly investigate' - as he put it – they may as well all pack up and go home.   The lady was quite forceful and told them they would do it the way she said and told the cerebral man "You and I will go and see ......" I didn't hear who - whilst the other two were to go though the documents.

The south-London boy seemed to capitulate at this point and offered that he would contact an old acquaintance that he used to work with to see what he could find out.

Everybody then seemed to settle down and the lady appeared more comfortable that she now had all three on board as to how they would tackle the project.

As I set them down the woman instructed the calmer man to settle the cab fare, which he did, reluctantly.   No tip.

meatvtskcirtwen

Guess Who Was in My Cab Today

9

I was winding my way through the crowds outside Buckingham Palace who were just dispersing having watched the Changing of the Guard. Most were tourists as was to be expected at this time of the year.

As I entered Constitution Hill a dapper man dressed in an old fashioned frock coat with sideburns and a barely recognisable moustache hailed me. He entered the cab somewhat sprightly but with dignity and asked in a gentle but clearly foreign voice to be taken to the Royal Albert Hall.

I continued along Constitution Hill towards Hyde Park Corner whilst he settled himself in the back enthusiastically taking in all around him.

"Do you have a time schedule, Sir?" I asked, anxious that if there was an appointment to be met we could make it in time.

"No," he replied, "I am going to look at the architecture of that fine building. I have a great interest in national landmarks particularly when they have been erected for some distinct purpose. The museums here in London are a wonder to behold; there has been much thought given to preserving the artefacts of your country and making them available for the ordinary man to visit and enjoy."

"You're here on a visit then, I gather."

"No, no" he replied, "I have lived here for some years. I first came here with my older brother from Germany where we had such a wonderful upbringing. I was fortunate that, at home, I was able to study under a private tutor who installed in me the values of education, most noticeably in the classics and arts. I learnt English, Latin and French but was especially fond of history, music and the natural sciences; I suppose that is why I take such an interest in the natural world rather than the people who control our lives."

"Do you have family here; is your brother still here - I'm sorry - I should not be asking you such personal questions. Let me rephrase that; how do you enjoy living in England?"

"I love England very much, I am privileged to be married to an English lady and we have a growing family to look after.   When I came here I was introduced to my future wife by my uncle who knew her family and thought that we would be a good match.   Also my brother, Ernst, was keen for me to meet her and accompanied me on that first visit."

He seemed to lapse into thought for a few moments and then added, "I remember the first time I met the lady who was to become my wife.   I don't think that she liked me very much to begin with and her annoying little dog used to jump up at me.   I think that it was when I began to play some of my own compositions on the piano that she became a little warmer towards me and we both enjoyed listening to Mozart and Mendelssohn."

"However, our children are growing and I must progress with my work on forging an exhibition that will be the envy of all countries. We are trying so hard to embrace many nationalities in a hope that it will encourage peace throughout Europe and the World but unfortunately politicians, as always, seek to impose their own agendas for something that is primarily for the people."

"Thank you Mr Cabdriver for your indulgence in listening to me.   I have such a short time to look around for I must be back in Windsor to see my wife and children this evening before 10.50 pm."

treblaecnirp

22

Guess Who Was in My Cab Today

10

Belgrave Square is a beautiful large square near Victoria where the real estate is exclusively owned by the Duke of Westminster. It houses a large number of Embassies and Consulates both in the Square itself and in the myriad of Mews at the back of the imposing mansions.

I was passing one such building, the Belgian Embassy on the corner of Halkin Place, when I was beckoned by an image of a man that was quite unique. He stood no more than 5.6" wearing a grey three-piece suit, a matching hat and a bow tie. There was a watch chain across his chest and a silver flower holder in his lapel. As he got into the cab I noticed that he wore spats and carried a cane surmounted by a silver emblem of a duck. However, the most striking thing was his carefully manicured and precise black moustache.

"Please to go to Scotland Yard," he said. "Very well, Sir" I responded, "you are aware that it is now on the Victoria Embankment having moved from Victoria Street" I added.

"Yes" he said, "I am going to see a detective friend of mine but this will be the first time in this particular building since they left the New Scotland Yard, I think, last year, *n'est-ce pas*?"

"Yes, that is correct.: I answered, "This building looks quite ordinary for what is probably the most well known of police forces throughout the world. You would have thought that the Metropolitan Police could afford something a little more prestigious"

"I have to be there at 11.45 am to discuss the matter that is most complicated" he said, and added "for me it is important to keep the little grey cells (tapping his head) always busy." He then gave a grin that was seemed intentionally restrained so as if not to disturb his magnificent moustache.

"Are you often in London?" I asked.

"I have a small apartment near Baker Street but I travel in the country helping where I can. You see I have a formidable brain for finding the truth and I am much in demand."

"Last week", he went on, "my services were required in your Sussex where there was a most unfortunate poisoning. For me it was not difficult. To look for that which you do not expect is the first rule."

"Then there was a case of the fatal stabbing of a Harlequin at a costumed Victory Ball. Chief inspector Japp sought my help and I was able to assist him find the killer because I asked for how long had the victim been dead."

"How can a simple fact like that have such a bearing on a case?"

"For me', he answered, "Everything is important and nothing can be ignored. To find the truth, *Mon ami,* one must turn over every stone and look into every hole. Assume nothing and discard nothing. Every little fact can be the arrow that points to the truth. From where did the knife come; did the shot that the witness heard come from the gun at the scene; from where was the poison obtained; at what precise time did the victim die?"

"There was the case where I, myself was present at the time of the murder. The method of killing was not as it was thought because I was distracted by a wasp but when I found the empty match box I knew of the false clue and I could then see the truth."

As we approached Victoria Embankment I timidly asked, "Have you ever been wrong?"

"*Mon Dieu!* I am never wrong" he spluttered, "You will permit me to get out here please." He gave me the correct amount for the fare and he was gone taking short ballerina-like steps in harmony with his cane with the duck's effigy thereon.

toriopelucreh

Guess Who Was in My Cab Today

11

I was driving along Bevis Marks in the City of London past the Spanish & Portuguese Synagogue that is over 300 years old, the oldest synagogue in London. Apparently, the outside was designed to look like a conventional English church to confuse would-be anti-Semites of the day from causing damage. Inside, however, the design was a replica of a mother synagogue in Amsterdam.

From my left came running out of an alleyway (previously known as Plough Yard where the synagogue sits) a man with an expressive face, bushy moustache and hair sticking out of his head almost on spikes giving an impression of someone who had recently been electrified. Although relatively well dressed I saw that he was not wearing socks and had a wildness about him, which might not have been so welcome on a dark night.

"Please," he said, " take me to the Embassy of Switzerland."

"Yes Sir." I greeted him and immediately planned my route along Bishopsgate, Great Eastern Street and City Road. "You seem to be in a hurry, have you an appointment to keep?"

"Yes, I am to give a lecture at 3pm and I would like to arrive in time to settle myself before speaking."

"No problem" I said whilst looking at the dashboard clock and wishing that he had given me a little more time. "Is it going to be a big audience?"

"I don't know; it is mainly to Swiss, German and American physicists and they are notoriously unreliable when it comes to attending professional assemblies."

"I am giving an explanation of the particle theory and the motion of molecules but no doubt someone will want to present themselves as an alternative intellectual and ask about the properties of light and my proton theory or my paper on the gravitational theory. You see, it was my statistical mechanics and my discovery of the law of photoelectric effect that led to the quantum theory that really started all this. One paper I wrote among many was on State of the Ether in a Magnetic Field. I was then awarded my PhD from the University of Zürich, with my dissertation on '*A New Determination of Molecular Dimensions*'."

"I would be quite happy to move away from these scientific areas and explain why I denounce nuclear fission but that is probably a bit beyond their imagination to see the wider concept of life."

I was totally lost by now and didn't have the slightest understanding of what he was talking about but not wishing to appear completely ignorant I asked, "Well, if you were to be asked at this gathering if there was another area of interest that you had what would be your answer?"

"Oh! Without doubt it would be music. I often think in music. I live my daydreams in music. I see my life in terms of music."

"And what guidance would you give to the young?" I asked.

"Simple," he answered, "Imagination is more important than knowledge. Logic will get you from A to B but imagination will take you everywhere."

I was relieved when we finally reached Montague Place and I set him down outside of the Embassy in good time. I have never worked so hard with a fare and I was, at this point, totally exhausted. So much so that I needed to go to the nearby cab shelter in Wellington Place to rest and recover.

nietsnietrebla

Guess Who Was in My Cab Today

12

I don't often take my cab out in the snow for driving becomes difficult and the traffic tedious.   Also, there is always a danger of other vehicles sliding into you and the slush of dirty shoes and dirty roads means a deep clean before the next day.

However, I had ventured out this day and found myself depositing a rather burley and sinister man at the Russian Legation in the police guarded Kensington Palace Gardens close to Kensington Palace.

About to move away I was flagged by man who had just left the nearby Nepalese Embassy.   As he approached I could see that he was very well prepared for our inclement weather dressed in a high quality anorak together with a fur-lined hood and thick snow goggles. His footwear was equally sturdy with knee-high strapped boots.

"Please to take me to the New Zealand Memorial at Hyde Park," he asked in thick accent that was difficult to place.   His request was accompanied by a wide engaging smile that lit up his whole face.

"Yes sir." I answered as I drove towards Kensington High Street.

Having seen that he was comfortably seated I opened a conversation by asking, "I see that you are well prepared for our season's snow."

"Yes," he said, "in my country we are used to heavy snow and we are always prepared for such weather.   Also, " he added, "my work often takes me into the mountains where, as a Sherpa, I lead groups in expeditions of climbing so I have an added responsibility of looking after them."

"That is something different," I offered, "how did you get into that line of work?"

"I was born in Nepal – although my son says that my birth place was Tibet – but no matter, in my country we have lots of people wanting to climb the mountains of the Himalayas and they must always have a guide with them for the mountains can be very, very dangerous. My father was a yak herder and I often went with him into the mountains so I started climbing when I was quite young.   I gradually gained sufficient experience to progress to a leader of the team or *Sirdar* as we are called.   Some years ago I was picked to be part of a team of some 400 mountaineers and helpers to tackle our 'Holy Mother' mountain that stretches five miles into the sky."

"It had never been climbed before although many had perished trying to do so.   Some had reached very close to the top but no one had knowingly succeeded.   In fact, the year before this attempt, I myself had reached within 1000 feet of the summit with a Swiss team but we had then to turn back.   This time, my sixth attempt, I wanted to be part of the two-man British team to finally conquer *'Chomolunga'* but I didn't get my chance until the first team selected had been forced to turn back to Base Camp because of equipment failure.   They had got to within 300 feet of the top."

"The expedition leader then said that the man from New Zealand, Mr Edmund, and I should go next which we did and finally succeeded in reaching the summit. Coincidentally, earlier on in that trip I had been roped with the New Zealander when he fell into a crevasse and I had pulled him out so we were good friends."

"So, did you ever go up *'Chomolunga'* again?" I asked.

"No but both my son, Jamling, and my grandson Tashi have conquered Everest.   Jamling did so twice, once, in fact, with Mr Edmunds's son Peter."

As I pulled in at the end of Knightsbridge I asked him, "OK, who was the first to step foot onto the summit, you or Edmund Hillary?"

"I have been asked this many times but when Mr Edmund and I were up there on top of the world we agreed there and then that we would never say who was first; we were a team, I made a promise."

As I watched this modest man walk into the Hyde Park Corner pedestrian underpass I had the feeling that I had just met a true pioneer whose accomplishment could never be matched.

gniznetaprihs

Guess Who Was in My Cab Today

13

It is a true but sad fact that not all cabbies will stop to collect a fare when the person is in a wheelchair. Sometimes, there are understandable (but not necessarily excusable) reasons why this should be so.   It may be the location, where to halt a cab for some minutes will mean congestion for other road users, or where the kerb is not conducive to loading a wheelchair.

Let me explain; to load a wheelchair it is necessary for the cab driver to unscrew and then pull out the loading ramp (situated only on the nearside) and fold up the rear seats to manoeuvre the chair; if the distance from ground to cab is excessive it will mean using an additional ramp.   Once aboard, the chair has to be arranged inside in a safe position and the seatbelts, including an extension belt applied to secure the passenger. This all takes time.

Most cab drivers never have a problem with taking a wheelchair user where possible and, in fairness to the disabled customer, they usually do not set the clock until all are loaded and ready to go.   Similarly, they will stop the clock on arrival and before unloading.

So, such was the situation when I was hailed outside of the Imperial College in the Exhibition Road by a man in the mechanised wheel chair.   "Good afternoon, Sir" I said, "Where to?"

"The Royal Society please, in Carlton House Terrace," he replied not in a conventional talking way but activated through some form of speech generating devise which gave a strange high-pitched computer type voice with an American accent.

"Yes, just a moment whilst I prepare the ramp ." I replied

There was no suitable raised pavement nearby so I had also to use the additional ramp to reach the ground to allow him to drive himself into the cab. His expert use of his machine gave him a safe entry and saved me from pushing him up the ramp.   He quickly settled himself inside and I was able to offer him the use of the seatbelt.

He was accompanied by a lady of about the same age and, I presumed, was probably his wife. Once he was settled I readjusted the passenger seats to accommodate her.

"Right, off we go then; Royal Society" I confirmed more for my own benefit than the passengers as I mentally decided on a route. "There must be a science connection here then," I volunteered.

"Yes" replied the wife, "another dinner and another speech on Black Holes. I have heard so many talks on Black Holes that I sometimes wish I could disappear down one myself." She looked at her husband and smiled condescendingly, "Don't you agree dear?" she asked him.

"Well, you know very well my dear," came this mechanised but perfectly audible response, "because I am a cosmologist this is bread and butter to me and these speeches help pay the bills."

"My husband", explained the lady "is forever being asked to address one society or another either here or abroad. One minute it is the Black Holes then quantum gravity and tonight the Higgs Boson and the Large Hadron Collider."

"How interesting," I offered, "then as a theoretical physicist I presume that you believe that the universe is governed by the laws of science rather than by God?"

"Absolutely," he replied, " there is a fundamental difference between religion, which is based on authority and science which is based on observation and reason. Science will win because it works."

"Well," I counteracted, "I am a creationist and I believe that God, or whatever you want to call him, was the creator of the Universe and it just didn't happen by chance. No matter how far you go back there has to be a cause of some type or other; even a Black Hole has to come from somewhere."

"I would have loved to have had the time to convince you differently", he said, "but we are here now and so we need you mechanical skills again." Once unloaded and the fare paid he drove his machine away., "God Bless." I called out mischievously.

The computer responded, "All I can say is Thank God I'm an atheist."

gnikwahnehpets

Guess Who Was in My Cab Today

14

I have always found the Norwegians to be a particularly pleasant nationality partly, perhaps, because of their close association with the British during the Second World War.

So when passing their Embassy in Belgrave Square I was more than happy to respond to a call for "Cab" shouted by a noticeably tall man who was just leaving. I would guess that he was possibly 6ft 6inches in height, if not more and despite his somewhat older years maintained an erect posture of a serviceman.

"Hello, Sir" I greeted him, "where can I take you?"

In his impeccable English he replied, "To the RAF Memorial on the Victoria Embankment please."

"Very good Sir" I responded and headed off towards Hyde Park Corner and Constitution Hill. "`I believe there is a memorial Service there this afternoon, is there not?" I asked.

"Yes, he replied, "it is the annual gathering of the Word War II Fighter Pilots' Association. There aren't too many of us left now but we still meet up every year if only out of respect for those pilots who never came back. What is interesting though when we meet is talking to the others and finding out what they are doing now."

"So what do you do now to pass the time?"

"Well I write, or rather try to but you have to have the right environment and circumstance to get the best results. I am lucky because I have an old Romanian caravan in my garden in Buckinghamshire where I can go and concentrate. Its proper name is a 'vardo' but everyone just calls it a caravan."

"Do you write about the War?"

"No, no" he replied, "I have always preferred children's stories but I have deviated at times into adult fiction and I was lucky to have some of my work unexpectedly televised a little while back."

"Tell me then," I requested, "How do you find the material on which to base your stories?"

"Ah well, you draw on life's experiences.   For example I went to a number of boarding schools as a boy and some of the horrible things that I saw there formed the basis for the darker children's stories that I wrote.   I even used some of the names of the pupils that I remember.   For example, there was a boy called Bruce Bogtrotter who was always eating cake so he got a mention in one story about a school."

"There was also the memory that I had of Cadbury's factory, which was nearby, sending us pupils 'taster' boxes of their latest chocolate bar inventions to sample before they decided whether to market them. That prompted another story.."

"My school life wasn't particularly pleasant but it provided a great source of material when I was writing.   I was once preparing a screen-play for another writer about a magical car and I was very excited about introducing a character who was a 'Child Catcher' complete with a horse-drawn cage into which the captured children were put."

"So are you writing anything at the moment that you can tell me about?"

"Well, actually, I am preparing instructions for my funeral, whenever that comes, for I would like to be despatched along with my snooker cues, a good bottle of burgundy and some chocolates.   And my instructions are that it should be a full Viking funeral in honour of my Norwegian parents."

As I set him down on the Embankment near the junction with Horse Guards Avenue I thought that, purely on the little he had told me about himself, his was a very interesting life.

lhaddlaor

Guess Who Was in My Cab Today

15

Driving along Cheney Walk I was hailed by an apparition of a man in what looked like 16th Century dress. He wore a long fur-trimmed cloak with a triangular black velvet hat on shoulder length hair and a heavy gold chain around his neck.

As I pulled alongside he said, "To the Tower of London please."

"Yes, Sir; anywhere particular - Traitors' Gate?" I joked.

"Ah. Once upon a time maybe." He light heartedly replied as he climbed in, "No, the main gate will be fine, I have a meeting to organise"

As we drove along I commented, "It's a pity that we don't have water taxies as in Venice, it would be much quicker and probably cheaper."

"That's true," he responded, " but I do this journey so often that I always allow plenty of time."

After a few minutes I said, "It must be very interesting to work in the Tower with all its history. Do you get time to look around?"

"Yes I do;" he answered, "In fact I work for a very old friend of mine and we are often there for one reason or another. But, I must confess things have become a little strained lately so I am not sure how long our friendship will last."

"How sad," I said, "It takes a long time to grow an old friend, as they say, and when such a relationship is ended it hurts everybody."

"Yes," he continued, "It really is over something quite silly. He wants to divorce his wife and marry a younger woman, which is a matter for him, but he also wants all his friends to signal their agreement. Some of us hold the view that he is wrong to be so hasty. Also, my wife died when we had a young family so I particularly find it difficult to accept the nonchalant way in which he wants to dispose of his wife."

"I have tried to keep my head down and not comment but he is something of a practical joker and the other night we were all together when he produced this scrap of paper saying that we all agreed to his divorce and a new wife and asked us, as his friends, to sign it.   Most joined in the joke and signed but I didn't and he took exception to this.   I tried to laugh it off but then he asked me directly in front of everybody, 'Will you sign or not?' I just remained silent."

"So what now?" I asked.

"Well, I guess our association will cool and I doubt if I will be working for him much longer.   It really is a great shame because we were very close and he often came to stay with me in Chelsea and I shall miss that.   However, I will not be pushed into doing something that I think is wrong no matter what the cost.   The sad thing is that even my daughter thinks that I am being a little bit stubborn and says that I should go along with it for the sake of peace but I just cannot; it has now gone too far."

"If only people could refrain from insisting that others agree with them then all would be well in the world but I suppose that would be Utopia.   Well, whatever happens I shall always hold him in high esteem; he has been a good friend for many years but my principles come first."

As we drew up at the Tower main gate I said, "It was nice talking to you. I hope that you are in good time for your meeting."

"Yes, thank you, I must get things sorted out before we start otherwise it will be my head on the block."

eromsamohttnias

Guess Who Was in My Cab Today

16

I was driving fairly sedately along Holland Park Avenue conscious that at the junction with Holland Park there was a statue, and probably the only statue in London, to a Ukraine saint by name of St. Volodymyr. It was erected to mark the 1000th anniversary of the Christianisation of the Ukraine (or Kievan Rus as it was then known).

Standing looking at a fresh posy of flowers at the base of the statue was a well built man of mature years who may, or may not, have just placed them there. He was holding his hat in his hands in a salute and I could then see a birthmark on his balding head. He had a round face and an avuncular air about him.

I slowed to a halt to allow a couple of taxis to turn right across me and at that moment the man saw me and waved. I turned left and stopped in Holland Park to allow easy access for him and as he came to the nearside cab window he said in a heavy accent, "I wish to go to see the Berlin Wall please."

"Do you mean at the National Army Museum in Royal Hospital Road?" I asked.

"I do not know where but there is some part of the Berlin Wall here in London" he answered.

Now not too many people know that there are several segments of this Wall both inside and outside of the Army Museum in Chelsea. Rumour has it that at the time of the fall of the Berlin Wall dividing east and west Berlin in 1989 some British Army 'Sappers' (or members of the Royal Engineers to give them their correct title) had decided that it would be a good wheeze to 'retrieve' some of the discarded panels from the Wall and bring them back to the Army Museum. Two of these panels can be seen on the forecourt there.

As I commenced the journey I asked my passenger "What makes you wish to see the Berlin Wall?"

He said rather slowly and with some thought to his use of English, "I am over here from Russia on a personal and private pilgrimage. You see for many years I was very involved in politics in the Soviet Union before it experienced *Glasnost* and *Perestrika,* of which I totally approved."

"The restructuring of the Soviet Bloc meant that the people of these satellite countries, and indeed Russia itself, could more easily determine their own futures and move away from the Communist ethos of control by the state. The idea that the State should own everything even down to the eggs laid by chickens on collective farms (where I have been) gave no incentive to the poor people to work for themselves."

"We, therefore, gradually eased back the involvement of the members of the *Politburo* in the day-to-day life of our citizens to give them a more meaningful control over their lives. It was not without its problems for some of these Members had been there a long, long time and were reluctant to change so we had to, shall we say, persuade them."

"And the Berlin Wall?" I posed.

"Ah well that is easy," he said, "The opening of the Wall to allow east and west Berliners to visit their families was the first step in this concept of 'openness' and once that had been allowed it was only a matter of days before those opposed to the segregation decided that the Wall should not stand at all."

"And your visit to the statue of Saint Volodymyr?"

"I am of mixed Russian and Ukraine heritage and half of my village starved to death in the Soviet famine of 1933. In addition, my dear, dear wife, Raisa, who was also from Ukraine, died not long ago. I have therefore come to honour her memory and those from my village who perished all those years ago."

"How very sad." I said as we drew up outside of the Museum. "The fall of the Wall and the resultant end of the Cold War was a massive global achievement and must have prompted consideration for the Nobel Peace Prize for those involved."

As he left the cab he said as an aside, "Yes, I have one of those but it will never replace my Raisa,"

vehcabrogliahkim

Guess Who Was in My Cab Today

17

It is hard to believe that the Embassy of the United State of America will relinquish its dominating presence in Grosvenor Square for a State of the Art modern building in Nine Elms.

The large and imposing gold replica of the American Bald Eagle that sits high above the portico will no longer cast its shadow over one of the most prestigious squares in London's Mayfair.

I was leaving the Square and heading for Upper Grosvenor Street when I was hailed by black lady who had just left the Consular section of the Embassy.

I pulled over and waited for her to cross the road towards me.

"Yes, Mam?" I asked.

"Could you take me to," she hesitated before reading from a slip of paper taken from her handbag, "the Equality & Human Rights Commission in Salisbury Square please."

'Yes, Mam" I repeated as I moved off towards Park Lane thinking as I drove, Constitution Hill, Birdcage Walk and along the Embankment'

Having decided on my route I saw that the lady was in her more mature years and dressed soberly but respectably. She sat quite upright clutching a brown handbag looking out at the passing buildings and becoming quite excited as we passed Buckingham Palace.

"Excuse me Sir," she addressed me in a slow deep south American drawl, "Is that where the Queen lives?"

"Yes, Mam" I replied. "And every morning at 11am you can watch the Changing of the Guard which is well worth a visit. I take it that you are visiting us."

"Yes," she answered, "but I am only here for a couple of days before flying home."

"Oh!" I said, "That's a pity because there is so much to see."

"I am giving a talk tomorrow evening to an invited audience of this Equality Commission on my experiences all those years ago in Montgomery when black people were second class citizens."

"Were you badly treated over something?" I asked.

"Yes, it was all very sad and demeaning. I was on a bus where, in those days, there was segregated seating. The white people had the front seats and the black people the rear seats. Also, if all the seats were taken a black person was obliged to give up their seat for a white person, even in the back section. I refused to do so when the conductor told me and there was an almighty fracas."

"In the end I was arrested and put in jail because I wouldn't obey the white person's law. Do you know that in my town of Montgomery in Alabama only white children were allowed to go to school by bus; black children had to walk. There were also separate entrances into stores for black and whites and I didn't think that it was fair."

"What happened then?" I asked.

"I was bailed out the next day and then we went to court where I was fined $10 but the case attracted a lot of publicity and there were protests and meetings and boycotts and everybody got involved. Then the politicians and the activists took it over. I received a lot of threats and lost my job as a seamstress in the departmental store. It was through this publicity that I met Martin Luther King when he came to organise the committee but I didn't really get on with him. In the end my husband said that we must move away which we did."

"Was that the end of your involvement?" I asked.

"No, not really for although it was difficult for me to find work I was hired as a secretary to a black US Representative and stayed with him for twenty years. They also gave me medals and things"

"I guess that this must have been quite traumatic for you." I said as I set her down in Salisbury Square.

"Yes it was but now I think that the funniest thing is that the very bus involved is in the Henry Ford Museum in Detroit and anyone, black or white, can sit anywhere in it, front or back". She giggled at the thought.

skrapasor

Guess Who Was in My Cab Today

18

The Science Museum in Exhibition Road, Kensington always has lots of people going in and coming out or just milling around so the official statistics that claim it has over three million visitors each year is quite believable.

It is often a rich source of work for the London cabbie either from the nearby rank or in the wider vicinity.

I was about to drop off a fare at the Imperial College further up Exhibition Road when a tall gentleman in his 60s and looking tremendously fit came to the cab and waited patiently for my passenger to alight and pay.   He then asked me in clear American accent if I could take him to the Apollo Theatre.

The first question to anyone asking for the Apollo Theatre is, " Do you want the Apollo Victoria or the Apollo in Shaftesbury Avenue?"

"I'm not sure" was his reply, "I have the ticket here" and after a slight hesitation read, "Shaftesbury Avenue."

Heading off towards Hyde Park Corner via the South Carriageway of Hyde Park this American gentleman thanked me for establishing which theatre he needed and asked, "How do you get to know all these places like theatres and cinemas and restaurants?"

I explained that the comprehensive 'Knowledge' that cab drivers have to pass gives a very good grounding for that but they still have to keep up to date.

Sensing that he was wishing to engage in conversation I asked if he was in London for long.

"I have a few days before moving off to Europe so I thought that I would catch a show.   I have spent the day at your Science Museum which I found tremendously enjoyable, and looking at the Space Capsule that is there took me back many years."

"You see, when I was young I graduated from college in aeronautical engineering. I was then granted a scholarship and trained as a navy pilot as part of that scholarship. I flew lots of missions in Korea and when I left the service I joined an organisation that was the precursor to NASA hence my interest in Space matters."

"So," I asked, 'What about these claims that you sometimes hear about the Moon Landing being a hoax?"

He laughed, "Oh I know how that came about. The Press were getting a bit excited over this rumour and at one Press Conference they went on and on to one of the astronauts who did actually land on the Moon and he eventually lost his cool and said, 'Alright, Yea, it was a all a wind up on a film set' and they believed him and ran off to file their 'Scoop'."

"I suppose that today we would class that as 'Fake News'" I offered.

"Well, it was certainly that, I can tell you, because I know for certain that the Moon Walk really did take place. In fact, I have the diamond studded astronaut pin that was taken to the Moon as a tribute to those three astronauts who died in a cabin fire during a launch rehearsal for the first Moon mission."

As we turned into Shaftesbury Avenue I said, "We are here now but may I ask you one final question? Why didn't the astronauts do more tests and bring back more rocks?"

"Well," my passenger answered, "They did bring some minerals back and much more was collected with later missions but the primary purpose of that first Moon Landing was to land on the Moon and return to Earth."

"Thank you for an interesting conversation" I said as he paid his fare. "Enjoy the show. What show is it?" I asked as an after thought.

"Oh. It's H G Well's 'First Men in the Moon'" he answered with a twinkle in his eye.

gnortsmralien

Guess Who Was in My Cab Today

19

For some unknown reason I have always remembered the location of the Theosophical Society's premises. Situated in the Bayswater Road at the junction with Gloucester Place, I had never ever seen anyone come out of a premises that presented such a dark and dingy image.

As I waited at the traffic lights at the junction adjacent to the building a somewhat small man wearing a sort of toga, or dhoti as I now know it to be, and a shawl came out of the building and across to me. He was in sandals and wore round 'pebble dash' glasses and a greyish moustache. His head was bald.

"Please could you take me to the Inner Temple" he asked.

"Yes, Sir," I replied, "please get in and make yourself comfortable."

When he had settled I said, "You must be the first person I have ever seen at the Theosophical Society. What exactly is it?"

"It is a non-sectarian body of seekers after Truth, who endeavour to promote Brotherhood and strive to serve humanity," he said. "I joined it soon after coming here from India to study law. I promised my mother that I would adapt English customs and go to dancing lessons etc. I was a vegetarian and through my visits to vegetarian restaurants I joined the Vegetarian Society and became acquainted with other members who invited me to come along to the Theosophical Society. So that is how I came to become a member."

"I am not sure that I would still be as welcome now as at the beginning because one of their precepts is not to involve the Society in any political disputes and I am afraid that for much of my life I have been just that; involved in political disputes."

He carried on, "You see after I became a barrister at the Inner Temple I was invited by a commercial company in South Africa to act as their legal advisor. I was only with them for one year but whilst there I saw much discrimination against the Indian communities who were attempting to register their civil rights. For example, my people were not allowed to vote, or to ride in buses or to use the sidewalk; they had to walk in the road.   I also suffered, and although I thought of myself as British, it was clear that others did not.   I stayed on and helped to form a political organisation for Indians to combat this lack of civil rights.   We founded the Natal Indian Congress and even volunteered to serve in the Boer War as an Indian Ambulance Corps. When the British declared war against the Zulu nation we tended to the wounded on both sides."

"I was there for over twenty years before I was asked to return to India by the leader of the Indian Independence Movement to help further the aims of Indian National Congress to secure independence for India.   That was a long and tortuous struggle and came to a head when the British declared war on Germany without consultation. We unilaterally declared independence.   Whilst we were subsequently arguing with the British Raj a group called the Muslim League were convincing the British, against our advice, to form a separate state for Muslims.   Then the British Government granted independence but with our country split in two, Hindu India and Muslim Pakistan.   This culminated in mass two-way migration of Hindus from Pakistan to India and Muslims from India to Pakistan."

"The history of India is beset with many difficulties.   When the Indian National Congress first pushed for independence it was never envisaged that it would result in India being split into two.   We had lived relatively amicably between Muslims and Hindus."

"In my own way I was faced with going along a path that I found hard to accept or to offer some form of non-violent objection.   I often staged protests by self-denial.   I would lead hunger strikes or other public actions of non co-operation and more than once found myself in prison for my beliefs.   At one point I spent two years in prison and was only released because of illness and I don't think that the British wanted the country to see me die in prison."

"Eventually our independence as a nation was secured and we endeavoured to move on despite the problems."

As we drew to a halt in Tudor Street I asked my passenger, "After all that how would you like to be remembered?"

"If I was to be presumptuous I think that I would like to be remembered as the Father of my Nation or, perhaps, for someone to write a song about me," he said.

ihdnagamtaham

Guess Who Was in My Cab Today

20

Soho Square is a delightful section of Down-town London that embraces a myriad of interesting buildings including the renowned St Patricks Church on one side, a French Protestant Church (in which the Huguenots found asylum) on another and in the corner of the third side is the Headquarters of 20th C Fox.

It was under the portico of this Georgian style building that I saw, standing between the four pillars, a young woman with a distinct head of platinum blond hair and wearing a white flowing dress that the wind was catching causing it to billow up around the lower part of her body. As she struggled to hold her modesty in place the Commissionaire waved at me to come across.

He said to me, "Please take this lady to Harley Street, she has an appointment there." He then held the door of the cab for the lady to enter and once settled I moved off confirming Harley Street as the destination and establishing the house number required.

"What time is your appointment?" I asked.

She answered in a clear American accent, "Oh! About two hours ago but no worry, he'll wait. My agent kept me longer trying to get a better deal. My 'shrink' knows when he is on to a good thing so he's not going to be difficult, not like some of the creeps I have met in my life."

"I gather that you mean in the film industry." I offered.

"You bet, honey", she replied, "this game is full of them and they are always waiting to screw you down but they have to be a lot smarter with someone like me who has come up the hard way."

"You know, ever since I was born I have had to deal with low-life and there are none so low as in the movie industry. I have been in foster homes and orphanages; I have been married three times, the first at sixteen, and had numerous encounters with others in the film world.

"One husband insisted that I converted to Judaism so to please him I did – for a time. I used to tell him I was the only Jewish atheist." She laughed.

She continued, "At the other end I have played opposite some well known stars, Cary Grant and Marlon Brando to name just two and have been given all sorts of awards, but, and this is the big but, they all use you for their own ends – what's in it for them – and when they are done they just cast you aside."

"How sad," I commented, "and you have to stay?"

"Honey, as I said, when you come from a beginning like mine you have little choice. I started off modelling and tried to get into films but it was hard going. I have been in Playboy and other magazines but they regarded me as a 'dumb blond'. I had a tremendous number of fans in the US Army and this kept me going. It was then that I decided to change to my mother's maiden name and that seemed to work. After some bit-parts in lots of films I hit it tops and in one year I had three box-office hits which was a good pay-roll but then the lean years come along and you have to struggle."

"I guess that it was in those lean years that I needed some help from pills. Don't get me wrong, it was nothing serious just something to pep me up a bit although I did do too much at times. I have been in rehab and under so many shrinks that I can't tell you just how many. At one time I found myself in a padded cell; that's how low I fell."

"And now?" I prompted.

"Well, there's no business like show business" she almost sang, " and look at these Honey," she said proffering two hands sparkling with diamonds, 'These are just some of my earnings – 'I guess you know that they're a girl's best friend!"

As I turned into Harley Street she said, "Would you be so kind as to set me down over there by the *Bus Stop*. That show meant a lot to me"

eornomnyliram

50

Guess Who Was in My Cab Today

21

Westminster Tower Gardens is a delightful green space adjacent to Black Rod's Entrance at the west end of the Houses of Parliament. It is a popular spot for lunch hour pick-nickers in the summer and an increasingly common location for TV news interviews of politicians.

As I passed by a middle aged lady came out of the gate and beckoned me to stop. She was somewhat tall with a sophisticated air wearing an ankle length full-skirted dress and carrying a parasol.

"Yes Mam," I greeted her.

"Please take me to the Brompton Cemetery," she said.

"Very good, Madam, " I replied, "do you want the Old Brompton Road or the Fulham Road end" I asked, "Oh, the end near to Earls Court Exhibition Centre please," she answered.

Heading off towards Victoria she commented to me that she had just been to a small meeting and wreath laying ceremony in the gardens next to Parliament and was now off to meet some more friends for another short ceremony in the Brompton Cemetery. She volunteered that, " Although I was born in Manchester, my later life had been in London where there was so much work to be done to help the workers who have been so badly treated, especially the women."

"How did you become involved with that?" I asked

She replied, " When I married my husband, who was a barrister, much of our life was in the north and that's where out children were born. My husband was what I suppose today you would call a 'human rights lawyer'. We came to live in London some years later and, through his work, I became more and more conscious of how women and girls were being mistreated not only in London but in Manchester too. For example, in the workhouses of Manchester little girls were being made to scrub stone floors and in London, the older girls were so badly treated at their workplaces that in Bow, the Bryant & May's factory which employed 2000 young girls, had a strike over their conditions."

"You see, women did not have the vote in those days so there was little they could do to alter things. That really convinced me that we needed some organisation to bring the things to notice. I formed the Women's Franchise League that sought to petition for women to have the vote. We had several other groups after that but all had the same aim, to secure the vote for women. We held meetings and marches and on one occasion 5000 gathered in Hyde Park for a public demonstration."

"There was so much opposition and mistreatment of those who protested publicly that there were all sorts of physical confrontations. Windows were smashed and graffiti was daubed on walls. Policemen were assaulted when they intervened and lots of the women were arrested. I was sent to prison several times after we chained ourselves to public buildings but we were forced to resort to active disobedience to be heard. In prison, we went on hunger strikes and some of the ladies were 'force-fed' which was horrendous."

"I later formed the Women's Social and Political Union which was independent of any political party. You see I had tried to join the Independent Labour Party that had been founded by Keir Hardy who was a friend but I was rejected because I was a woman. I did eventually join and later on even joined the Conservative Party but this was because of the advent of Bolshevism. All we wanted was for women to have a say in how our country was run and for us to have equality in public life. It has been a long struggle."

As I set her down at the cemetery entrance she giggled, and said, "Of course the press, who were sometimes for and sometimes against us, always looked for silly little things put in their papers. I remember that they wanted to know when I was born as if this was of any importance. I was actually born on the fifteenth of July but I told them that I was born on the fourteenth of July so they could write a story about my kinship with the female revolutionaries who stormed the Bastille." She went away smiling at this memory.

As I drove off I reflected on how some people had struggled to achieve what we now regard as the norm.

tsruhknapenilemme

Guess Who Was in My Cab Today

22

Carlton House Terrace at the southern end of (Lower) Regent Street comprises two blocks of John Nash's creations built in the mid 19thC on the old Carlton House site.

I had dropped off a fare when I was called by a man who had just come out of the Royal Society, that is situated there. "I would like to go to St. Mary's Terrace, Maida Vale please, the southern end."

"Yes Sir" I answered in acknowledgement as I turned into Pall Mall mentally planning my route. "Are you on a time schedule?" I asked.

"No, no. I'm going to look at some sculptures there. I have just come from a symposium where a colleague suggested that I might find it interesting to see these steel statues."

"Is that your field of interest?" I enquired of him.

"Not at all," he said, "I am a cryptanalyst and I specialise in theoretical computer science. In fact, the whole of my life has been taken up with this science in one shape or another. I left Cambridge with a pretty good degree and I was asked to work for the Government to develop their emerging computer programme. As a result I was involved in and created a machine that was used for decrypting signals. It was called a *bombe* and had been originally developed by the Polish but my design allowed us to use a crib-based decryption system which quite dramatically cut the time needed to decipher the messages of enemies."

"There were other related fields in which I was involved. We were at war with Germany and the interception and interpretation of their signals was of paramount importance. Our work was, of course, extremely confidential and involved all sorts of cerebral contributions but finally we created the 'Enigma' machine that gave us a valuable advantage in knowing what the Germans were planning."

"The naval messages were the most difficult to break but by the use of my electromechanical machine, which gave us the facility for careful tuning and adjustment, we succeeded in severely reducing the naval losses on our side by the interception of their plans."

"I wrote several papers on the subjects in which we were involved but one of the most interesting projects was the ability to encrypt and decrypt speech using a secure voice communicating machine that I developed. I used one of Churchill's speeches to demonstrate its value. I was also keen to address the problem of artificial intelligence and began by writing a chess programme for the stored programme computer on which we were working."

"One of my earliest interests was in Mathematical biology and I published what I regard as my best work, a paper called 'The Chemical Basis of Morphogenesis' which is all to do with the development of patterns and shapes in biological organisms."

"In truth, many of my colleagues considered me somewhat strange. I was a long distance runner and missed out on an Olympic place for the Marathon by eleven minutes. I also used to suffer from hay fever so it seemed quite logical for me to cycle to work wearing a gas mask. At work I wanted to keep safe my own tea mug so when I wasn't there I would chain it to the radiator. What they could not understand was my approach to remedy a problem with my bicycle chain. It would come off every so often so I used to count how many pedal rotations I could make before it next came off. In this way I could stop and adjust the chain before that happened."

"Well," I interjected, "I am amazed at how anybody could even start to formulate a system that could address this business of deciphering and encryption. I am absolutely useless at puzzles of any kind. The Rubik Cube baffles me and as for Solitaire where you have to remove all the marbles on a board but leave one in the middle is just mind-boggling. I have yet to get even close to solving it."

As we drove along St. Mary's Terrace he said, "There. Over there by that steel statue is fine, thank you." I pulled to a stop and he settled the fare. He then said, "Look, take this and when you get home have a go at the Solitaire using this formula. I created it for my niece some years ago, you just have to commit the sequence to memory."

He strode off loudly whistling Tom Jones rendition of 'Delilah'.   What a strange but interesting man, I thought.

gnirutnosihtamnala

Guess Who Was in My Cab Today

23

The Royal Opera House at Covent Garden had always held a fascination for me; first because it has that mystique about it that shouts privilege and opulence and secondly because the historical Bow Street Police Station directly opposite is the only police station where the traditional blue lamp is replaced by a white light. Apparently, Queen Victoria gave the directive when she visited the Opera House and was dismayed at the dinginess caused by the police station lamp.

As I passed by reflecting on these two thoughts I saw a crowd of musicians outside the Opera House (they were carrying various musical instruments) and from the group emerged a very large man with a black beard in a tuxedo complete with a white bow tie.

He waved at me and as I pulled over he said in a heavy Italian accent "I woulda lika to goa to a Hyda Parka."

"Yes Sir," I replied, "anywhere in particular?"

"Yes", he said, "I would like that part where they hold the open-air concerts."

I decided that The Strand heading towards Pall Mall and Constitution Hill was the best route and off I set. On the way I asked him, "Have you had a good evening?"

"Wonderful," he said, "I love Covent Garden, it has that air of magnificence about it and whenever I come to England I always come here. Many years ago I did go to Wales for the Eisteddfod, in fact I won a competition there but that was a long, long time ago."

"So, I guess that you are an opera singer" I ventured.

"Oh yes, I love all sorts of opera but my favourite composer is Puccini. When I first started singing with my father, he was a baker in a town called Modena in northern Italy, we sang *La Bohème.* and I have preferred Puccini ever since. Music was never my first choice and when I was a boy I really loved football and wanted to be a goalkeeper because I played football all the time but my mother said I should become a teacher so I did but then singing took over."

"So how did you move into music?" I asked.

"As a boy we were very poor, four of us in two rooms and then I went to work on a farm. When I became a teacher I started singing under a personal trainer and went for seven years for formal vocal training. Also, I would go to see Mario Lanza films and come home and practice in front of the mirror. At one time I had bad trouble with my voice and gave up singing but when I recovered I found that my voice was even better than before. It was also at this time that I developed a breathing technique for my singing that has been so valuable to me ever since."

"So, have you been all over the world to sing?" I enquired.

"Yes, and I have seen lots of very poor people just like I once was. It is so sad to see the children suffering so I have set up some foundations in the poorer countries that try to help them. I also arranged a competition for promising young singers and took the winners on an international tour; in China we played to an audience of over 10,000 people. We have played benefit concerts throughout the world and the one aria that they always want me to sing is *Nessun Dorma*, for, I suppose, they watched the football World Cup when it went world-wide and became the biggest selling classical record of all time."

"What is it about Hyde Park that takes you there this evening? Surely, there is nothing on there tonight" I asked.

"I had a great friend that I met at a concert in Hyde Park and now she has gone I just wanted to come back and remember her at the place where we first met. She was a beautiful lady but she died tragically in Paris, another favourite, now sad, city of mine. I was asked to sing at her funeral but I could not sing with grief in my voice so I declined; but I did go to the funeral. "

"How would you like your name to be remembered" I asked as we stopped.

"Here at Hyde Park I dedicate to my lovely Princess my favourite aria, *Nessun Dorma* in which is the line, 'My name no on shall know'.   That is how I would like to be remembered"

ittoravaponaicul

Guess WhoWas in My Cab Today

24

Not infrequently cabbies are asked to go outside of the centre of London. It is not always a popular request for getting a fare back to 'Town' is unlikely. However, I had been to Gypsy Hill and was on my way back when passing the public school, Dulwich College, I was hailed by a heavily build man with a ruddy complexion. He was in formal dress and wearing a number of medals on both the right and left chest (the right side for awards from a foreign country) and a ribbon around his neck that I recognised as that of a Knight Bachelor.

"Yes Sir," I greeted him, "Where can I take you"

"To the Royal Geographical Society, Kensington please." He answered.

Elated that I was going to earn a fare for going back into London I planned my journey and contemplated how I could engage my very distinguished passenger in conversation.

"Have you had a good day?" I asked him.

"Yes, very nice, thank you. I have been to my old *alma mater* for a Presentation Day and I am now off to the Geographical Society for dinner with some of my old travelling companions; we meet up every two years, or at least those of us who are left do, and we reminisce and plan our next adventures."

"I see that you are a Knight of the Realm so how were you awarded your knighthood and these other medals?"

"Well, it certainly was not for my academic ability at school. I left at sixteen and became 'an apprentice before the mast' on a sailing ship and after four years progressed to Master Mariner which meant that I could command any British ship."

"But today I suppose I could best be described as an explorer. It was always my desire to be part of the first expedition to reach the South Pole. On the first occasion I sailed under Captain Scott and three of us set out on foot and reached the southern-most point ever achieved but we didn't reach the Pole. On our journey back to the 'mother-ship' I became very ill and subsequently the captain sent me back home to England. I think that I could have carried-on but he would hear nothing of it but then we didn't get on terribly well. However, I did experience my first balloon flight which was amazing."

"The second trip was really to heal my wounded pride at having been sent home on the first occasion. This time I led the expedition and we went even further south but the journey was very difficult and we had to turn back before reaching the Pole; we were near to starvation and on half rations but even then I decided that a suffering member of my crew should have an extra ration of half a biscuit. The highlights were that we were the first to climb the Antarctic's Mount Erebus and also to discover the approximate location of the South Magnetic Pole."

"When we returned home they gave us a hero's welcome and that's how I came to receive a knighthood and other awards. I immediately started planning a third attempt. I needed lots of sponsors to raise the money and also to see how Captain Cook's latest attempt was progressing. However, in the meantime the Norwegian, Amundsen, reached the South Pole so I had to rethink my plans.   I decided to change it to be the first land crossing of the Antarctic Continent."

"This time the ice beat us. Our main ship, *The Endurance*, was crushed by pack ice and I had to abandon ship.   We lost our supply boat which was blown from her moorings and the crew had to be rescued. We camped on the ice for several months before we took to an open boat and sailed 800 miles to South Georgia."

"Since returning home I have been with the North Russia Expeditionary Force and also as a volunteer in command of a troop ship in South Africa.   I have tried politics and journalism and there have been other missions but I am still drawn to the Antarctic."

As we turned into Kensington Gore I asked him how much he regretted not being the first to the South Pole.

"A live donkey is better than a dead lion," he answered.   "I did not achieve my goal of being the first to the South Pole but now I am about to embark on a fourth expedition which will be to circumnavigate the Antarctic Continent.   I leave next week in my ship, *The Quest,* starting from Rio de Janeiro.

notelkcahstsenreris

Guess Who I Wasn My Cab Today

25

The BBC is an institution that appears always to have been with us. The monolithic building in Portland Place seems to cast its shadow over the whole of England. Whenever I pass by I look at the myriad of persons entering and leaving, the flamboyant and the ordinary, the celebrities and the unknown, the 'would-be' and the 'has-beens'. It is as if this great headquarters is the father of everybody who has ever served the media.

My recent pass-by identified a rather ordinary man who called me to take him to Frith Street. Nothing memorable about him at all except for a soft Scottish accent that had clearly been adulterated by years out of the country of his birth. Having confirmed his destination I drove on down Regent Street for the short journey via Oxford Street and Soho Square.

"How has your day been?" I asked gently to see if he was of a mind to talk.

"Very well, thank you," he answered, "I have just been to a meeting at the BBC to progress some ideas that I have been working on. You see I originally created a semi-mechanical analogue system that was capable of transmitting moving silhouette images – in other words television. Others then got into this field but my invention was ahead of them although in fairness we all benefitted from each other's work."

"Strangely enough, I built the first working television by utilising some oddments including a hat box, some darning needles, scissors, a tea chest and some glue and sealing wax. It was very rudimentary and at first just transmitted a grey scale image of a head at five pictures per second then we increased to 12 pictures per second and I was able to convince the Royal Institution to let me give them demonstration from my laboratory in Frith Street."

"Not long afterwards I moved into colour transmission by using a number of scanning disks. My next experiment was long-distance transmission between London and Glasgow although the Americans were doing the same between New York and Washington. I then set out with my own company and soon made a transatlantic link between London and New York. I also made a television programme for the BBC and tried drama, a theatre television system and even an outside broadcast of The Derby and a boxing match. We were using what was called the thirty-line system but I then moved to a 240 line and on to a 405 line. I was working on a 1000 line but a big fire in my, other, laboratory at Crystal Palace ended all that and the BBC went to another dimension."

"However, I later developed the cathode ray tube with a revolving disk of colour filters which was taken up by two companies in the States and so we went on to where we are today."

"Have you experimented with any other inventions?" I asked.

"Some" he answered, "although not always successfully. I tried making diamonds from heated graphite but only managed to short out Glasgow's electricity supply. I made a razor from glass that was rust resistant but easily smashed. Then there was the pneumatic shoe, the thermal under-sock, fibre optics and an infrared night viewing device. Even during my television experimentation I gave myself a 1000 volt electric shock; fortunately my only injury was a burnt hand."

"Now, I just dabble. My health has not been particularly good and I recently moved to Bexhill-on-Sea for a better climate so I come to London less often."

As we arrived in Frith Street I said, "After all this work how would you like to best be remembered."

"Oh! I guess that it would be nice if someone, sometime was to tell the story of my life but it would, of course, need to be a television programme and would have to start with a grainy image of me and gradually move into full colour with very high definition. "

driabeigolnhoj

Guess Who Was in My Cab Today

26

The Temple Bar memorial pedestal which represents the boundary between the City of London and Westminster is located in the middle of the road where The Strand becomes Fleet Street. This was the principal ceremonial entrance to the City of London and was, in earlier times, a gatehouse and barrier to regulate trade into the City.

The City of London has always jealously guarded its independence from Westminster amid claims that The Magna Carta granted such distinction. In truth, there is evidence that since the early 13thC there has been some form of autonomy granted to the City and even today the Sovereign, no less, will pause at the Bar to seek permission from the Lord Mayor to enter the City. Only the Sovereign ranks above the Lord Mayor when within the square mile.

It was as I passed by this monument that I was called upon by a tall gentleman in a long coat and a very distinctive 'stove pipe' hat. He was very smartly dressed and carried an air of authority and prominence about him.

"Yes Sir," I greeted him, "Where to?"

"Ah!" he said, "I would like to go to number 4, Whitehall Place please."

"Number 4, Whitehall Place, that used to be the original Scotland Yard did it not?" I suggested.

"You are quite right cabbie," he replied, "in fact that was the actual address for the Headquarters of the Metropolitan Police when it was first formed but because the public entrance was at the rear in a street called Scotland Yard that name became synonymous with this 'New Police'".

"May I ask why you call it the 'New Police?'" I enquired.

"This was the name by which they were known in the early days to distinguish them from the old 'Charlies' and watchmen that used to have the responsibility (but not the commitment) of keeping law and order in London.   As Home Secretary I could see that the policing system in London was in need of reorganisation so I recruited 1000 men of specific characteristics including height, presence and integrity to carry out this role. I insisted that their uniforms with silver buttons and a belt were of blue, rather than the red of the army, and that they wore a 'stove pipe' hat like mine so that they could more easily be seen and recognised in public.   The hat later mutated into a helmet with a chinstrap to secure it. They had a truncheon, a rattle (which later was changed for a whistle) and handcuffs."

"I must say that the whole idea did not go ahead as smoothly as I would have wished.   For example, I had earlier formed the Royal Irish Constabulary in Ireland without any difficulty whatsoever but when I first introduced this Act to Parliament the City of London 'Godfathers' who sat in the House of Commons threw it out because they didn't want any change to their little conclave.   It was for that reason that when I reintroduced the Bill a couple of years later the City were purposely left out and we passed the Act for the rest of London.   The City didn't get their Force until ten years later and have stayed separate ever since."

"That wasn't the only hiccup.   On the 29th September when the 'New Police' started half of those I had recruited didn't report for duty and of those that did a good number turned up drunk so I dismissed them straight away.   Thereafter, I had to weed out the unsuitable or criminal element and it was several years before we managed to have a respectful band of officers that the public could trust.   Once that was established I pushed for all cities in Britain to have a police force."

"Looking back, do you have any regrets?" I asked.

"Not in the formation of the police."   He answered.   "But I do regret that an attempt to assassinate me ended up killing my personal secretary whom a madman mistook for me; that was sad."

"And how would you wish to be remembered?"

"Well, when I was 21 I was elected to Parliament by every one of my constituents, quite unique - mind you it was in Ireland and there were only 24 of them!   Other than that I think that I would like a public house or two named after me; that would be quite original. Thank you cabbie, here at Scotland Yard will do nicely."

leeptreborris

Guess Who Was in my Cab Today

27

Queensgate Gardens is a rather select square of Kensington just north of the Cromwell Road and a stone's throw from the Natural History Museum. Not a natural cut through but cabs will often be seen depositing fares here.   I had done just that when I was called by a gentleman who was just leaving one of the houses.

He was quite distinguished and was wearing a khaki uniform of the First World War together with puttees and medals.   He wore rimless glasses and was smoking a pipe but it was the dog collar that caught my attention.

"Good afternoon Reverend, where can I take you?" I asked.

"I would like to go to the church of All Hallows by the Tower" he replied in rather clipped but perfect English.   Do you know where that is?"

"Yes, Sir." I confirmed, "Just opposite Tower Hill."

"Thank you," he said, "I have a service to conduct there in one hour for ex-servicemen.   The house that I have just come from used to be a meeting place for us in the early days and every year about this time I meet up with some old friends from the services and we don our old uniforms out of respect for those young men who died during the Great War wearing the same uniform."

"So Queensgate Gardens is important to you?" I volunteered.

"Yes," he said, "The story really started in Belgium near Ypres at the beginning of the First World War when a clergyman friend and I decided that these poor soldiers needed a place for rest and relaxation before going back to the Front. We wanted to offer a Christian alternative to the debauched area of the local town.   We rented a dilapidated house and repaired it and over time we converted the loft into a chapel and provided lots of tea and comfort for the men.   There was also a library but to stop the books 'walking' I insisted that each lender left his cap behind as surety - no soldier would ever dare walk out of the house bareheaded!   By a strange coincidence the house was opened on the 11th November that first year, a date that has now become so poignant in history"

"Everyone was welcome irrespective of rank or position.   One of the most popular ideas was the Noticeboard where the men could leave notes asking as to the whereabouts of friends or read messages left for each other.   We called it Talbot House in memory of my friend's younger brother who died at the beginning of the conflict.   But, of course, soldiers being soldiers they soon referred to it as 'T H' that then became 'Toc H' following the then British Military Signalling Regulations. i.e. T for Toc. "

"After the War there was still a demand from these men for somewhere to meet and relax so using the well known title of 'Toc H' we opened a Service Men's Club in Queensgate Terrace and then expanded to other towns, and indeed countries.   I was particularly pleased to open one such Club in Australia where I was born and lived for two years.   We became, in effect, an International Christian Movement."

"We then decided to buy Talbot House and moved all the contents temporarily to my church of All Hallows until we finished the work. Everything was then placed back in Talbot House which is now open to the public."

"Some years later, during the Blitz, even my own church was bombed so I had to find funds to renovate that but in so doing I recognised that the East End of London, where my church was located, itself suffered from harsh and impoverished conditions.   With the help of the American Ambassador we not only rebuilt my church but also did a lot of work in the East End."

Just before reaching the Tower of London I asked him, "Out of all this misery and need was there anything that you remember that makes you smile now?"

"Well," he answered, "In Talbot House we had all sorts of men from every walk of life and some needed to learn how to live in a social setting.   We had a particular problem with one form of behaviour so I put up a notice that read, *'If you are in the habit of spitting on the carpet at home, Please spit here.'* That brought a few smiles and solved the problem."

"Thank you Cabbie for a nostalgic ride, please keep the change."

Guess Who Was in My Cab Today

28

Tucked away near the Hilton Hotel in Park Lane is a small road called Hamilton Place that houses two more prestigious hotels. It also hosts the Royal Aeronautical Society that is a professional institution for those engaged in the field of aerospace. Hamilton Place is a convenient short cut into Piccadilly or back into Mayfair.

I had just dropped off at one of the hotels when an airman in full uniform left the Aeronautical Society and signalled for me to stop. As he climbed into the cab I saw an array of medal ribbons on his chest, some of which I recognised as World War II awards and one that I knew to be the distinguished Flying Cross but with a Bar. He also had the Wings emblem above the medals signifying a pilot.

"Yes Sir, where to?"

"I would like to go to the RAF church, St Clement Danes, in the Strand please," he answered, "I have a memorial service to attend." As he settled in I saw him pull out a pipe and began to suck on it vigorously.

"Have you had a good day?" I asked. "Yes, OK," he said, "but some of these people that you have to mix with are so pathetically reticent to say or do anything that might upset the apple cart. God forbid that we have another war with these so-called leaders in charge; they would still be looking up their own backsides whilst the enemy advanced."

Assessing that here was a man of character and fearful that he might go into a rant I said, "I see that you are no stranger to active service."

He answered, "And that's what these people need, to be out in the thick of it and realise that not everything can be achieved through strategy and planning. Often you have to fly by the seat of your pants, forgive the pun, and act on instinct. I managed to come through the last war with those principles and even when I was shot down I continued to baulk authority in trying to escape until I was sent to Colditz."

"I guess that you are not one to give up easily then?" I commented.

"Well no. Before the war when I joined the RAF and first started flying the authorities put a ban of low-level aerobatics but being me I went against that and did a slow-roll near the ground and crashed. As a result I lost both legs, one above the knee and one below. I was lucky because I was given two false legs and managed them well enough to walk, dance and play some sport. I successfully passed the re-test for flying but I was still discharged from the RAF as unfit. When the war came I immediately applied to re-join and I suppose because of need I was allowed back to fly in combat."

"I see that you have the Distinguished Flying Cross with a Bar. That was obviously during the War. But what is the other Medal with the Bar?"

"The Cross is awarded for bravery and was for action during the Battle of Britain and the Bar to that came for my sorties over France. The other medal is the Distinguished Service Order and Bar and these two were awarded for leadership in combat. In fact, all four awards came within twelve months over 1940 and 1941. I was doing alright at that point but then I was shot down over German occupied France and finished up as a POW where I remained until the Americans released us at the end of the war."

"So how did you manage to get out of the aircraft with your disability?"

"That was a bit traumatic because as I was going down one of my legs got trapped and I couldn't get out. Fortunately, the wind drag got hold of me and sucked me out snapping the stay that held my false leg in place."

"And after the war?" I asked.

"I went back to work for the Shell Company and eventually finished up as Managing Director of Shell Aircraft. They had been very good to me and given me a job when I was first invalidated out of the RAF so I felt that I owed them something. It also allowed me to continue flying for many more years."

"And how would you like to be remembered?" I enquired.

"Well, I have had my false legs for over 50 years so I think that I would like one to go to the RAF museum as an incentive to other airmen that you can do anything if you have the will."

Guess Who Was in My Cab Today

29

India House in the Aldwych is a large 1930s building sitting alongside Bush House (once home of the BBC) and Australia House where, in the past before parking restrictions, Australian expatriates tended to congregate in their motor caravans.

This home of the Ambassador for India displays on its outer shell the emblems of its twelve states under British rule.   One might be surprised to find the Swastika depicted on the Bihar and Orissa state decoration.   This, now hated symbol of Nazism, was originally an ancient religious icon that, in Sanskrit (the sacred language of Hinduism) meant 'well being' or prosperity and good fortune.   Sadly, in the 1920s it was adopted as the symbol of the German Nazi Party.

So in passing slowly in traffic it was no surprise for me to be hailed outside of this edifice by lady in a sari.   She was small with a weather beaten and deeply lined face that was framed by her sari of simple white cotton with a blue border.   She carried just a small purse.

"Yes Mam" I greeted her, "Where can I take you?"

She answered in strong accent of the Indian subcontinent, "Please take me to Kentish Town, to the church of Our Lady Help of Christians."

Thinking quickly the most direct route for me was all the way round the Aldwych and up Kingsway and through Camden Town.

As she settled in I asked, "Do you have a time to be there?"

"Oh," she said, "I am giving an address later tonight at that church so I have plenty of time."

In my rear-view mirror I could see that she was avidly taking in all around her.   "Are you a visitor or do you live here?" I asked.

"Oh No" she replied, "I am visiting our Mother House in Maida Vale but I have first to meet with a dear priest friend of mine in his parish in Kentish Town.   I promised that when I was next in England I would come to Mass in his church and talk about my work.   It will also be an opportunity for me to meet with one of your Princesses who might be there."

"So what is this work that brings you all the way to England?"

"Well, it is a long story but when I was eighteen I left my home in Albania and went to Ireland to become a nun with the Sisters of Loreto.   After about one year I was sent to India where I continued my studies and took my vows at the Loreto Convent and became a teacher at the convent school.   It was whilst there that I became more and more aware of the abject poverty among these poor people.   They really were the poorest of the poor."

"I opened houses for the poor to live and receive treatment and medical help and, for those close to death, some comfort in their final hours.   I wanted to provide some help for the hungry, the naked, the homeless, the crippled, the blind, the lepers and all those who were unwanted and uncared for."

"I suppose that I was outspoken at times but that is often the only way to engender some action by the authorities.   They frequently criticized me claiming that our houses were unhygienic and that I was promoting a cult of suffering.   They became even more abusive because I would speak openly against abortion."

"They claimed that the money spent on these poor people should have been used for palliative care of the sick.   But I just wanted to help as many people as possible in whatever distress they encountered.   We opened a leper hospice in Calcutta and provided out-reach clinics providing medicine, dressings and food.   We wanted these people who lived like animals to die like angels – loved and wanted."

"How do you raise the money needed for your work?" I asked.

"The money mainly comes from charitable donations but also from the Indian government, the Catholic church and many other sources. As an example, I was awarded the Nobel Peace Prize for the work of the Missionaries of Charity in our endeavours to overcome poverty and distress.   I would not agree to the banquet that is usually held but I did accept the $192,000 on the proviso that it was given to the poor of India. Also, people will often give a small donation to our sisters when they pass them in the streets be it here or in India or anywhere that we have houses. Everything goes towards the care for those who have nothing."

"How long have you held this desire to help others?" I enquired.

"Since I was about twelve I felt myself drawn to missionary life. When I left Skopje to go to Ireland I knew that I would never return, indeed, that was the last time I ever saw my mother and sister."

"So, when you return to Calcutta what will be your next task?"

"Only God knows the future. I must just follow his will and do what he wants of me."

As this very spiritual lady left the cab I declined the fare and asked that she donate it to the poor in India. She thanked me on their behalf and pressed into my hand a small silver medal. I learned later that this was a Miraculous Medal that she often gave out. It was, in effect, her 'calling card'. I felt highly honoured and treasure it to this day.

Guess Who Was in My Cab Today

30

I was heading for the International terminus at St Pancras Station looking for a meaningful fare. As I reached Acton Street junction with Gray's Inn Road I saw a large man, well over six feet tall come running out of the Water Rats public house waving at me.

I stopped and in he jumped, "Please take me to the Palladium" he asked in a west -country accent with a hint of Welsh. "I have a show to catch and I stayed longer than I should have."

As we drove off I could not help but notice on his left lapel a gold emblem of what looked like a rat. "Ah", I said, "unless I am mistaken you must be a member of the Grand Order of Water Rats. Is it right that, once a member, you always have to wear that emblem?"

"Yes" he laughed. "and if you are caught by a fellow Rat not wearing it you must pay a fine which goes to charity. When I was King Rat I used to fine my colleagues heavily if they were reported to me and I intend never to be on the receiving end and have to pay money."

"So how do you become a 'Rat?' " I asked him.

"The numbers are limited to two hundred and, by and large, it is restricted to those in the entertainment industry. You have to be nominated and seconded and all that type of thing and generally need lots of support from other Rats."

"Why a rat?" I asked.

"The Water Rats were formed just before the 1900s by two music hall entertainers who kept a racing pony. It was quite successful and they used the winnings to help impoverished colleagues who fell upon hard times. One day they were taking the pony home in the pouring rain when a bus driver shouted out, "What you got there mate?" They said of their bedraggled accomplice, "It's our trotting pony". "More like a water rat" he quickly replied and the answer stuck."

"What's on the bill tonight then?" I enquired.

"Well, I do conjuring tricks but they don't always come off not that it matters too much for I get as many laughs when they go wrong.   I do sometimes slip in a trick that does work and that seems to please them all the more.   I started off when I was in the Army in North Africa and my stage entrance was always the 'Sand Dance' wearing a pith helmet which seemed to get them giggling and then I went into my routine.   One night I forgot to take my pith helmet with me so I grabbed a fez off the head of a passing waiter and it nearly brought the house down so I stayed with it.   When I was demobbed it was natural for me to continue in the entertainment business."

"It must be great fun to see people laughing at your show."

"Laughing is infectious," he said, "And even at rehearsals when you don't have the flow of the show the fun is there.   I remember one afternoon rehearsal for 'Sunday Night at the London Palladium' when there was a policeman in the wings watching.   I suppose that he had slipped off his beat for a break and was watching my act.   The tears were streaming down his face and he was almost doubled up with laughter and then his helmet fell off and that creased me up.   It so reminded me of that old Charles Jolly music hall song, the Laughing Policeman."

After a few moments he asked me, "Do you like marshmallows, I love them; I could eat them all day long; I even dream about them.   Last night I dreamt that I was eating a massive ten-pound marshmallow. When I woke up this morning the pillow was gone." He gave that double laugh.

As we pulled up at the stage door of the Palladium he paid me the exact fare of £8.60 and then as he was about to walk away said, "Here, have a drink on me" and poked something into my pocket.

When I looked in my pocket later I found he had given me a tea bag!

repoocymmot

Guess Who Was in My Cab Today

31

Salisbury Square is a rather serene looking small block of offices just off of Fleet Street and within a stone's throw of the Inner Temple Inns of Court. One could be forgiven not noticing its position when taking a cut-through from Holborn *en route* to the Embankment.

It was as I drove down towards Dorset Rise that I saw the strange sight of a man of about 30 years wearing a long raglan type brown top coat with a white ruffled cravat and a very long and full brown wig that came down well below his shoulders; it was the type of hair worn in the 17th Century that was then known as a 'powdered wig'.

I pulled over and he got into the cab and asked to be taken to Tower Hill near Trinity Square. Anticipating that he might be going on a history ramble I suggested that I could drop him at the Tower Hill site of executions in the mid 16th Century.

"Yes, that's fine, thank you:" he answered, "I am just going to have a walk around the area and reminisce   There is so much in that vicinity that takes me back to my earlier years. My father was a tailor and my mother the daughter of a butcher but we also had an MP and a Lord Chief Justice in our family. Much of my early days were spent there and, in fact, I was baptised in the church of St. Bride's just off Fleet Street and went to school, first in Huntingdon and then at St. Paul's."

"When I started work in the Admiralty my office was in Seething Lane and I also lived nearby and it was from there that I saw and recorded in my diary the events of the Great Fire of London. I had kept a diary for several years just to record my daily life. I noted down political and social occurrences but also much of my own personal life. I recorded my jealousies, my insecurities, my concerns about everything including my relationships with my wife who was from a respected Huguenot family, and even my own medical problems."

"As it was never intended for publication I could be totally open and honest particularly when referring to the various ladies that came into my life. I was a great supporter of Olive Cromwell, perhaps because of our mutual affinity with Huntingdon. I was present at the execution of Charles I and also on the ship that brought Charles II home from the Netherlands. I returned to being a Royalist after Cromwell's death and, in fact, was present at Charles II's Coronation. It is all recorded in my diary including my thinking and my reasons for acting as I did."

I could not help but bring him back to the Great Fire of London. "So how came that you saw so much of this occasion?" I asked.

"Well, I was asleep in my house in Seething Lane when my servant woke me to say that there was a big fire in the Billingsgate area. My first thoughts were that it should not concern me, as that area was where the poor lived close together and also that the various outbreaks of the Plague usually took place there because of the living conditions. I went back to sleep but later my servant, who had obviously been monitoring the fire said that over 300 houses had been destroyed and it was still going on. I went up to the Tower and, in fact, climbed on to the roof of All Hallows by the Tower church to watch. Then I went on to a boat on the Thames to get a better look and came back and started collecting all my valuables together in case it came nearer."

"I had certain relationships with both the Royal Court and also with the City of London and, at the behest of the King I convinced the Lord Mayor that he had to demolish houses in the path of the fire to create a wind-break. He was reluctant because he didn't want the City to have to pay for re-building but the high winds and the absence of any means of fighting the fire with water convinced him and he finally agreed. In the end it took three days to control and then came the looting and rioting. I was that worried that I sent my gold to London for safekeeping. Thankfully, my house was secure but my clerk lost everything. Most importantly, my diaries were safe."

"So, do you still keep a diary?" I asked.

"No", he answered, "I had maintained it for some ten years but then my eyesight began to fail and I was afraid of going blind so I stopped the diary. I sometimes read parts of it and reflect back and wish that I had been able to continue but my health was not good at that time so I chose to finish."

"What was your last entry?" I enquired.

"I think that I just said that I was going to bed." He replied.

Guess Who Was in My Cab Today

32

I was driving along Denmark Street, or 'Tin Pan Alley' as it is affectionately known, reflecting on how a small street in London's West End, barely one hundred metres long could command such historical proportions in the music industry.

Named after Queen Anne's husband the street developed into a central point for all aspiring musicians and which, since the 1950s, has housed musical instrument shops, recording studios and café's where the inner circle of this genre of entertainment have gathered to ply their trade. The 'Melody Maker' and 'New Musical Express' were both born here and it has consistently attracted those individuals who believe that the more outlandish or bizarre their attire the more chance they will have of making it in the music world.

It was no surprise, therefore, to be hailed by a man in his early thirties dressed in a complete white suit with multi-coloured buttons sown everywhere. It had a large stand-up collar suppressing an even larger white shirt collar. On the back of the jacket was the motif of an eagle similarly marked out. The clean-shaven face of its wearer had long, thick sideburns and a mass of black hair that seemed to dance about his head.

As he climbed into the cab he asked, quite politely, in a southern drawl, "Say, could you take me to the home of the Ambassador of the United States?" The pronunciation of the word 'Ambassador' seemed to take as long to say as the rest of his sentence.

"Yes, of course I answered" and then somewhat mischievously, "Is he expecting you?"

He laughed and replied, "Well, whenever I visit a foreign country I always like to pay my respects to my President's representative; you never know when you might need him."

"Do you travel a lot?" I asked.

"Yes, I am in the music world and since I was in high school I have tried to make it as a singer and guitar player. It's not been easy, in fact when I was at school my teacher told me that I had no aptitude for singing but I think that she just didn't like my type of music. I failed my music exam and it wasn't until I entered a school talent competition that I really found my way forward. I oiled my hair and grew my sideburns and developed a style of singing and presentation that was a bit different."

"I then started going to music stores and listening to all kinds of recordings but I think that it was the African/American artists that inspired me most. I went to many different establishments; white gospel singers, Blues venues and other segregated places as well as listening to radio shows. I was encouraged to cut some tapes and get some interviews with groups as a singer, but no deal. One professional bandleader told me, 'Stick to truck driving boy because you aint never going to make it as a singer'."

"After one late night recording at Sun Records we were about to go home when I started messing around with my guitar and playing the fool. I launched into a Blues number and was jigging and gyrating and the others joined in. Suddenly, the head of the company heard us and put his head round the door and shouted to start again and record the piece. When the track was played on the radio people thought that I was a black singer or some 'Hillbilly'. The rest is all history."

"When we finally got to perform in public I was accused of threatening US security by arousing sexual passions in teenage youth by my gyrating and style of performing. At one gig the National Guard were called to support the police in case of trouble. We had some fun and on one occasion I sang "Hound Dog" to a basset hound that I had dressed in a top hat and a bow tie!" He laughed at the memory.

"I was then called for military service and spent two years as a GI but during the time I was away my manager released various songs that I had previously recorded and had ten top-forty hits so I was kept in the limelight. Sadly, whilst on service my beloved mother died and whilst going through a particularly difficult time I was introduced to amphetamines and became hooked."

"When my military service came to an end I was given an honourable discharge with the rank of sergeant and sent home but the train was mobbed at every station and within one month I had recorded another album. I always wanted to get into films and used my experience to produce 'GI Blues'. I went on to make twenty-seven films but none really made the big time, they were really just the vehicle for my music so I went back to concentrate on singing."

"They tell me that my appearance on an Ed Sullivan show had an audience of sixty million viewers and I was voted the best selling single artist. At a Las Vegas show I had a standing ovation both before and after my act so I guess you can say that I made it big-time in the end. Not bad for a guy who kept being told that he couldn't sing." He laughed again.

"So what are your future plans?" I asked.

"I have never performed outside of the US or Canada so I am here to look at that possibility. But," he added, "There *has* to be a purpose ... there's got to be a reason ... why I was chosen to be who I am. There are any number of impersonators of me, be it look-alike, sound-alike or just hobby copyists. I guess long after I'm dead there will be someone who mimics me enough to make others believe that I am still alive. As long as the 'Royalties' keep coming I don't give a damn," he said with a smile.

As I dropped him at the gates of Winfield House he sauntered off singing, "Love me tender, love me sweet, never let me go ...."

Guess Who Was in My Cab Today

33

I was resting in the serene and hidden Charterhouse Square near Smithfield's Market when I was approached by a distinguished gentleman wearing the uniform of a British Army officer around the time of the Boer War. As part of this uniform he sported a Stetson hat and a neckerchief. Tall and thin with a bushy moustache he was every inch the colonial man. He wore the insignia of a colonel and was carrying a large sketchpad.

I hastily put aside my half-eaten sandwich as he drew near and asked in a clipped and public school accent if I could take him to Westminster Abbey.

"Yes, of course", I replied. Then added, by way of a means of opening a discussion, "That's a beautiful building that you have just come from, worthy of a drawing?"

"It has great memories for me" he said, "That was my old public school of Charterhouse before it moved to Godalming in Surrey. Originally, it was a Carthusian Monastery before being 'sacked' in 1535 when Henry VIII brutally martyred nineteen Carthusian monks from there in his pogrom against the religious life. Every year we remember those martyrs."

"I have just been there doing some drawings in the Master's Garden. There probably is not a day when I don't sketch something. Both my father, who was a Church of England vicar, and my mother, who was the daughter of an admiral, were keen artists. I never really knew my father for he died when I was three so I guess all that I have achieved in life stems from a very strong mother."

"In my early days I had an all round experience in music, yachting, drawing in pen & ink, canoeing and, most importantly, living off of the land where I would stalk, trap and cook game. When I was commissioned into the Hussars I served in South Africa and also as an intelligence officer working out of Malta. On some recognisances I would portray myself as a butterfly collector to hide my real identity."

"In my time abroad I saw several theatres of war and was in command at the Siege of Mafeking which went on for over 200 days. My orders were to prevent our large stock of supplies from falling into the hands of the Boers and whilst I had the option to destroy the stock and the ability to escape with my men I decided to hold out until relief arrived.   My mounted officers were forced to kill their animals for food and the Mafeking Cadet Corps of white boys were magnificent in helping me deceive the Boers into what we were doing.   The fact that I had the son of the Prime Minister under my command was an influencing factor."

"I had several postings to Africa (at one time I was the youngest Colonel in the Army) and once met a US scout who was attached to the British Forces.   It was through him that I took to wearing a Stetson hat and a neckerchief; the neckerchief had several purposes; it prevented sunburn on the neck, it served as a triangular bandage for first aid and also displayed an identifying feature by its colour and design. "

"Whilst in Africa I wrote a military training manual 'Aids to Scouting' that became a best seller but then when I returned home I found that teachers and leaders of youth organisations had adopted it so I re-wrote it for the younger generation.   It was partly through the obedience displayed by those boys of the Mafeking Cadet Corps that I was minded to start up the Scout Movement here at home.   I brought the neckerchief and Stetson hat into the uniform along with a 'woggle' to save tying the neckerchief.   Each troop had its own scarf with colours as an identity.   I then arranged a camp for 28 youths on Brownsea Island in Poole and found any number of identical scout camps cropping up everywhere.   My subsequent book, 'Scouting for Boys' sold over 150 million copies."

"I am very proud of the Scout Movement and of being its first Chief Scout.   Within two years of our first Scout Jamboree in 1920 we had a million scouts from thirty-two countries and that soon rose to 3.3 million.   At our first Scout Rally at Crystal Palace a number of girls turned up in scout uniform so my sister and I decided to give girls their own Movement; they became the Girl Guides."

As we pulled up outside Westminster Abbey I asked, "What now?" He hesitated before answering and on the misty glass panel behind me he drew a circle with a dot in the middle."   I looked quizzically at him. "That, in 'Scout trail language,' means 'I am going home'." He said, "Goodbye cabbie."

llewop-nedabdrol

Guess Who Was in My Cab Today

34

It was dark on an evening in early autumn as I was passing the Shepherds Bush Empire intending to head back into town.   There was a piercing whistle and I looked around for the caller.   Suddenly in the gloom I could just make out a man dressed completely in black waving at me from near the stage door.   He was heavily built and wearing a black Stetson type hat and a long black leather topcoat that reached almost to the ground.   He was carrying an equally black guitar case.

"Yes sir," I greeted him, "where to?"

In a deep south American accent he said, "I would sure like to go to your Wembley Stadium but first I need a drink, can I get a drink around here?"

I said that I would stop at a petrol station on the way where he could buy some beer.   This seemed to satisfy him and off I headed towards Wood Lane.

"Do you have to be there at any particular time?" I asked,

"Well, I have a concert to perform which will go on until 2am and then I am going on home for the last time."

"Is that back to America?" I enquired.

"Yep, sure is," he said, "I have been on a tour of Europe and I just now want to get back to Nashville, Tennessee to my dear wife June. Normally she would have been with me on this tour but she has had some heart problems so she stayed home."

He then went on, "We've been married over thirty years and have done a lot of gigs together, we both write songs but she has written some of the best.   We have performed at the grandest of places both here and in America but strangely the best receptions have been when we played in prisons.   I guess the inmates there appreciate a free concert and identify with me although I have never been in prison – well not really.   I have spent a few nights there for misdemeanours but nothing serious."

"Anyway, these prisoners get real excited at these visits especially when I play their own song.   I wrote *Folsom Prison Blues* and played it there.   They went wild when I sang the line, 'I shot a man in Reno just to watch him die….' Because I guess they identify with my lyrics."

"I wrote another song for San Quentin Prison and played to the prisoners there.   You can guess that lines like, ' 'San Quentin, I hate every inch of you …'   and 'San Quentin, may you rot and burn in Hell' just brings the house down."   Now you might think that this is hardly conducive to good order there but you have to appreciate that my lyrics are to show that I understand their feelings; they are paying the price for their crimes and somebody has to stand alongside them."

"It's the same with the native American.   They have been suppressed and trodden on, their lands taken and their dignity shattered.   I stand for them as well and have recorded songs about their plight.   And who is there to remember those thousands of young soldiers that have died in all these worthless wars.   That is why I wear black, because I mourn for those we have rejected; that is why my songs are often about injustice and sadness.   Even novelty songs like 'A Boy Named Sue', written by a friend of mine and recorded live at San Quentin, are there to highlight unfairness."

"You see, I have come a long way since I worked in the cotton fields of Arkansas and these scars on my hands are as a result of that.   My mother bought me my first guitar and I learned to play sufficiently well enough to stand alongside Willie Nelson, Carl Perkins, Jerry Lee Lewis and Elvis Presley.   I always thank God for all that I have and, despite my other faults, I have never denied my faith.   I regularly proudly profess my beliefs with my good friend Billy Graham at his crusades and sing of my love of the Lord.   I am a Christian, maybe a troubled Christian but still a Christian"

"I have had some rough times in my life.   At one point I thought that I had Parkinson's but it turned out to be autonomic neuropathy associated with my diabetes.   I have been in and out of rehab and there have also been times when I could no longer draw the crowds to my concerts.   In my heyday I once played to a crowd of 12,000 at a town called Lafayette – the town population only numbered 9,000 – and then when things were really bad to just 350.   I had to do commercials to stay alive.   And when I was down even my pet ostrich that I kept on my farm kicked me.   That was painful."   He grimaced at the thought.

"So, apart from your songs, how would you like to be remembered?" I asked.

"Well. I have written over 1000 songs but I have always liked trains and I have written about them quite often in my time but I would like 'Engine 143' to be my epitaph; that was a great song.   Anyway, I guess that I have already reached immortality because there was a black tarantula found at Folsom Prison and named after me."

As I pulled up at Wembley Stadium he looked around him and said, "Just thinking about what you said about being remembered, you know, I am going to donate my tour bus, 'JC Unit One', to the Rock and Roll Hall of Fame.   That should do it."

He paid his fare and said, "Thank you sir " as he strode off to another concert.

hsacynnhoj

Guess Who Was in My Cab Today

35

Driving along the elevated section of the A4 in west London towards Hammersmith one can see on the left the azure blue cupola of the Russian Orthodox Church in Harvard Road below. There are many small yellow suns depicted on the rotund roof and it is crowned with the three-bar cross of the eastern rite church. For a fleeting moment it resembles the flag of the European Union.

Further along the A4 I was interested to see a man gesticulating to me to stop. I was a little unsure at first as to whether I would welcome him as a passenger but my inquisitiveness got the better of me and I pulled in to the kerb.

He was a big man, some six feet tall, wearing a long dark and scruffy coat. He greeted me with a smile showing some black uncared-for teeth amid an unruly beard and a face that clearly had not seen water for many a day. His hair was equally unkempt but the most striking aspect of his face was the piercing blue eyes that stood out from his swarthy and dark features producing an almost hypnotic stare.

"Yes Sir" I enquired rather hoping that he really didn't need me or that his request was one that I could legitimately decline.

"I wish to go to the headquarters of your security services," he stated in a booming, guttural east European voice.

As he got in I asked if he wanted MI5 or MI6. "Yes" he answered.

Assuming that, being an obvious foreigner, he would likely have more business with MI6 than MI5 I mentally prepared a route down to the Albert Embankment.

Intrigued by this strange man I decided to try and engage him in conversation. "Do you have a time to be there?" I asked.

"No, no, they do not know that I am arriving but I have to tell them something about Russia" he all but snarled.

"Might I suppose that you are Russian?" I continued.

"Yes, I was born in Siberia in Pokrovskoye into a peasant family and I was the only one of my seven brothers and sisters to survive. It is very hard in Siberia with no schooling and no way to get a better way of living. I was following a bad life of drinking, stealing and disobedience to authority that could only be bigger trouble."

"I got out only because I had gone on a pilgrimage to our St Nicholas monastery and became friendly with a theological student and some of the elders or *starets* as we call them. I began to travel around with them and found that people needed someone to whom they could turn to resolve their spiritual crises or other problems. After a while I came to be known as a *strannik* - a holy wanderer or pilgrim – in whom they could confide and my reputation grew throughout Siberia as a mystic who was able to cure many of their ills."

"I was friendly with a number of church leaders and they gave me some letters of introduction to a seminary in St Petersburg where I met the priest who was the confessor to the Tzar Nicholas and his wife, the Tzareen Alexandra. By now I had been mixing with church and social leaders so I had a good following, particularly among the ladies. They would privately tell me their troubles and I would privately help them in whichever way I could."

"One day the Tzareen asked to see me to confide her worries about her only son, Alexei. She told me that he was a haemophiliac and was in great pain. I went to see him and prayed over him and told his mother that he would be free of pain the next morning. He was. This happened several times and I was able to help on each occasion. I was given freedom to the palace and I became known as Alexei's healer. The Tzareen was very grateful and when the Tzar was away with his military I would be there to comfort the Tzareen and her daughters."

"My close relationship with the Romanov family upset a lot of the senior advisors and more distant members of the royal family. They accused me of being too close to the Tzareen and of being a charlatan. They spread rumours that I used my position to accept bribes and sexual favours from my admirers. Even the Holy Synod of the Russian Orthodox Church, with whom I long had a strained relationship, accused me of immoral and evil practices and said that I was a threat to the Empire."

"I gradually became aware of a plot to kill me but they do not know with whom they are dealing.   I am a very strong man and I can resist any attack on me.   Someone once tried to poison me but I cannot be hurt; I am a man of God.   I will return to St Petersburg and continue my work as a faith healer and confidant to the rich and powerful.   I am protected."

As we approached the Albert Embankment I asked him how he had stopped little Alexei's pain when all the doctors had failed.

He said, "The doctors and their prognosis only added to the distress of the Tzareen and her son and I needed to overcome that.   Over the years as a wandering monk, I had developed the art of hypnoses and this was my method of treatment by first easing the worries of the boy's mother and relaxing her.   In so doing Alexei became more calm.   Those who would criticize my methods chose to forget that spiritualism and theosophy were widespread in Russia long before I came to St Petersburg.   The people were ready for me."

As we pulled to a halt he paid the fare, shook my hand and, very strangely, asked if I had ever heard the music of Bony M.   We parted with what I thought was a very respectful "Proshchay."

nitupsarirogirg

Guess Who Was in My Cab Today

36

The headquarters of the Freemasons, or The United Grand Lodge of England as they are officially called, occupies a large and imposing stone building in Great Queen Street, Holborn.   Built in the early 1920s it was dedicated as a memorial to the 3000 or so masons killed in the First World War and, it is claimed, occupies a site has been associated with Freemasonry for close on 250 years.

Passing by I was hailed by an intriguing looking small, pale and thin gentleman wearing a fine white wig that had rolled edges at his ears. I guessed that it dated from around the late 18th C. He was strangely dressed in a bright crimson high-buttoned long jacket with a ruffled cravat and matching ruffled cuffs.

Speaking with a distinct north European and somewhat squeaky and high pitched accent he asked me to take him to the Royal College of Music in Prince Consort Road, Kensington.

As he settled himself I asked if he was a visitor to London.

"Yes," he answered, "I am here very briefly and I wanted to visit the Grand Lodge of England but also to see again the autographed score of my Piano Concerto that the Royal College of Music hold in their archives."

"You see," he continued, "I have been composing and playing music since I was very, very young.   In fact, I used to play the *clavier* or keyboard, as it is now more often called, with my sister under the guidance of my father.   My father was composer and teacher to the Royal Court of Salzburg and, as my teacher, he thought that I had an unusual talent and introduced me to the Salzburg Court of Joseph II where I was engaged as official musician."

"My father then took me on tours and I played to many of the Royal households of Europe; I suppose that they thought it somewhat different to be entertained by a child prodigy.   I was playing my own compositions some of which I had created when I was no more than five or six and I wrote my first symphony when I was eight years old."

"We went to many of the capitals of Europe and it was when we were in Rome that I first heard Allegri's Miserere. I was fourteen at the time but, attached to this piece of work, is my own personal story. Gregorio Allegri was a singer in the Sistine Chapel in the Vatican and composed this particular piece some hundred and fifty years before I heard it. The Pope of the day was so impressed that he forbade on penalty of excommunication for anyone to copy the score. He allowed only three copies to be made; one for the Holy Roman Emperor; one for the King of Portugal and one to be held by the Italian priest of the Vatican responsible for sacred music."

"When I first heard it sung by the Sistine Chapel Choir I was totally captivated and, aware that no formal further copies would ever be made; I committed every single note to memory and returning from the Chapel I immediately wrote it down completely from my memory. I went back a couple of days later to hear it again just to make some finer adjustments but that then became the first unauthorised copy ever to be made. Within three months I was receiving congratulations across Europe for this piece of work. I was then called by the Pope (Clement XIV) who, I thought, was going to excommunicate me but instead he showered me with praise and gave me a medal."

"When I returned from Italy I was engaged as a court musician by the ruler of Salzburg, Prince-Archbishop Colloredo. He paid me very little and tried to prevent me from using my talents outside of his establishment. As a consequence I lost many paid performances. I eventually left and went to Paris but things were so bad that I was almost penniless, so much so that I had to pawn most of my valuables and borrow money from my Masonic friends. Then there was another lean period when I stopped composing and spent a lot of time playing the piano and writing concertos."

"I went to Vienna for a long time and, in fact, it was there that I wrote most of my 600 pieces of work. The Emperor gave me a lot of support with good commissions and a part-time position."

"I have met many distinguished people over my life; musicians, theatrical performers, aristocrats and royalty. I have written many religious scores, several operas and even dances and I have visited many Royal Courts to play my compositions."

"When I had money my wife, Constanze, and I had a very plush standard of living.   She was also from a musical family and sang in some of my compositions.   We had a very comfortable apartment and sent our son to an expensive boarding school.   We kept servants and the Freemasons, for whom I had composed some music, became an even more important part of my life. I enjoyed playing billiards and bought my own billiard table.   I also kept pets, including a dog, a starling, even a horse."

"But now I must concentrate on my Requiem.   I started composing it several years ago but I still have yet to finish this, my masterpiece, but I intend to work hard on it now. "

He paid his fare and said, "Thank you and goodbye."   With that this strange and clearly talented little man was gone.

trazomsuedamagnagflow

Guess Who Was in My Cab Today

37

The Victoria and Albert Museum is one of several beautiful buildings that lay within a short distance of each other in South Kensington. Built at the instigation of Prince Albert following the success of the Great Exhibition of 1851 it forms a trio with the Science and the Natural History Museums.

I was waiting on the cab rank outside of the 'V & A' (as it is colloquially known) just enjoying the sunshine when a tall, middle aged lady somewhat severely dressed in an ankle length tweed two piece suit elegantly descended the shallow steps from the main entrance.   Her hair was tied back in a bun and she wore a choker necklace.   She was carrying a battered straw hat.

"I would like to go to Bolton Gardens please" she greeted me on reaching the cab.

As she settled herself in I asked "Did you enjoy your visit to the V & A – don't you think that it is one of our finest museums - and no admission charge either."

"Yes" she answered, "I often come here just to visit the library and look at the wonderful collection of books.   I, myself, made some donations a little while ago and it is very pleasing for me to see others enjoying my contributions.   I never say anything to them, of course, that would be impolite."

Intrigued, I asked 'Were these donations of books that you no longer had a use for?"

"No, no.   I used to write a lot and also illustrate my stories but I had a whole series of drawings that were just gathering dust and becoming dishevelled so I looked for somewhere that they could be of use."

"You see, I came from a professional family – my father was a barrister and my grandfather an Member of Parliament.   Both sets of grandparents were from a fabric merchant background so we were comfortably off."

"I was educated at home by governesses right up to my late teens" she continued, "so consequently I did not have the lots of friends that children acquire now through school.   My friends were usually cousins with whom I corresponded by letter and I used to add some little drawings to make the letters interesting.   I remember one very ill boy that I used to write to and when I ran out of interesting things to say I made up a story about my pet rabbits.   I always kept lots of pets; there were rabbits, mice, a hedgehog, bats and butterflies and other insects.   I used to take them on holiday with me. "

"My interest in nature soon extended to drawing in microscopic detail various items from fossils to animals to plants.   I made friends with some botanists at Kew Gardens but because in my day a woman could not publish papers or even attend lectures I just used to give my drawings to various museums.   I then decided to try and have published some of my stories that I had sent to my ill friend.   I started with 'The Tale of Peter Rabbit' and went on to other stories about my pets but no publisher would take them on so I published them myself.   It was only because a long term friend, the Reverend Hardwicke Rawnsley, (who in fact started the National Trust) supported me and he influenced a publisher to take on my work."

"As a child I had always read an awful lot and became very interested in stories of fairies.   I also started illustrating children's fairy tales and then incorporated my various pets into other stories that I wrote. I started a diary and this influenced my story writing but I never spoke about my private life."

"My first book of Peter Rabbit was a great success and afterwards came 'Squirrel Nutkins and others.   I was publishing two or three books a year and even designed and patented a doll of Peter Rabbit so I suppose my genes of merchandise were always there.   I then became interested in farming and land conservation and this took over.   I helped my friend, Revered Rawnsley, with his National Trust idea and over the years I bought a number of farms and managed them myself to preserve their identity.   All in all, we gathered quite a lot of land for conservation."

"I was also interested in furthering the Girl Guides and allowed them to hold their summer camps in my grounds.   My true commitment, however, was to the ideal of the National Trust and I worked hard with the Reverend Rawnsley to make it a success."

"Well," I said, "we are now here at Bolton Gardens; anywhere particular?"

"No, just here is fine.   That primary school there is now situated on the spot where our house was.   I have so many fond memories of my early life here that I like to come back from time to time and reminisce.   Do you know that my last governess was only three years older than me and we still remain close friends.   I have sent her children many of my illustrations over the years; in fact the 'ill child' that I mentioned earlier was her eldest son.   I am sure that he still remembers 'Flopsy, Mopsy, Cottontail and Peter ' and who knows he might just be telling those same stories to *his* children."

Guess Who Was in My Cab Today

38

I have often reflected on how those bastions of the hotels, restaurants or departmental stores, the doormen or 'commissionaires', acquire the skill to emit such a loud whistle by the use of two fingers and their tongue. Or how they can so secretively and efficiently (and unseen by most) pocket the gratuity of their client for whom they have secured the services of a cab. Is there some kind of training course available or is it in their genes and are they called upon to demonstrate this prerequisite whilst being interviewed for the post?

One such guardian was a doorman at Harrods store in Knightsbridge. Irish by birth and imposing by nature his six feet four frame towered over his colleagues and customers alike. His resplendent and iconic Harrods Green uniform with gold buttons and braid was completed by a top hat with a broad gold band. His regular position was at the Basil Street entrance from where he could, via his whistling, summons a cab from the rank at Hans Road thirty metres away.

This particular doorman, whom I knew personally, once staged a one-man strike at his workplace over some domestic issue between him and the management. It went on for several days but was somehow finally resolved for he was soon back on his point to continue his services. I suspect that his Irish Guards experience may have been brought to bear on his adversaries.

On this Hans Road rank one afternoon this shrill summons from my Irish friend called me to his door and he deposited into my cab a lady of mature years dripping with pearls and fox fur. As he closed the door she said with a slight American accent, "To the Waldorf Hotel please."

'Yes Mam." I replied and added by way of polite conversation and subtly acknowledging her nationality, "I understand that the Waldorf was built by an American businessman who wanted to bring the US idea of hotels to London having built one in New York."

"That is very true," she said, "I can confirm that because that 'American businessman' that you speak of was, in fact, my father-in-law.   He built the first Waldorf Hotel in New York but there was some dispute when another member of the family built a second hotel next to it.   This row continued into who should adopt a certain name and my father-in-law decided to come to England and brought his son, now my husband, with him.   My father-in-law mixed in the right circles and did much charity work so much so that he was elevated to the House of Lords first as a Baron and then a Viscount."

"In truth, Walter is my second husband – I divorced my first and left him in New York - then came to England where I met Walter.   I had become part of the social scene in London as did he and, I suppose, both being Americans and both enjoying the aristocratic scene and, by chance sharing the same birthday, we became attracted to each other.   It did help, of course, that he was amazingly rich and was the Member of Parliament for Plymouth but we did have a happy marriage."

"When his father died, Walter succeeded to the peerage and had to give up his seat in the House of Commons so I decided to fight the seat and I won."

"So you became the first woman MP then?" I asked.

"That is not factually correct," she said, "I was the first woman MP to *take up a seat* in Parliament but the first elected woman MP was an Irish Sinn Fein candidate but she did not take up her seat   I don't mind being thought of as the first woman MP for I suppose whilst it may not be factually correct I was the first and only woman there for a while. "

"I didn't have a particularly smooth ride in Parliament; I never reached ministerial office but I did achieve some minor successes like the raising of the drinking age from fourteen to eighteen.   There were lots of prejudices against women and my position in the aristocratic social scene probably didn't help much.   I took great delight in telling some of these jumped up MPs that I was the daughter of a slave owner – my father had run a railroad business in the US by the use of slave labour before slavery was abolished. "

"When we married my husband's father bought us the Cliveden Estate in Buckinghamshire as a wedding present.   We had lots of lavish social functions there and most of the top people in the UK attended.   We had royalty and ambassadors and many of those high on the social scene.   I was accused by my adversaries of being anti-Semitic, anti-Catholic, anti-Communist and of favouring Nazism mainly because a number of my friends and associates became involved in the German 'appeasement' policy.   We were known as the 'Cliveden Set'.   Yes, I did have strong views on all these matters and no doubt I did make some mistakes but I was devastated when the Conservative Party (aided by my husband) caused my retirement from politics after twenty-five years.   Our marriage then drifted apart and we had other very sad family problems."

"Who do you remember most from those times?" I queried.

"Well, I suppose Churchill.   You see in those days I was regarded as being quite witty and always ready to speak my mind; as was he.   I often had cross words with him and once told him at one such exchange that 'if he were my husband I would poison his tea'."

"And what was his reply?" I asked.

She hesitated for a moment and then replied, "He said that 'If I were his wife he would probably drink it'."

She paid her fare and, escorted by another smart doorman, entered the Waldorf Hotel.

rotsaycnanydal

115

Guess Who Was in My Cab Today

39

Just parallel to the doctor's conclave of Harley Street lies the small but select Wimpole Mews.   The early purpose of these mews dotted around the more expensive parts of Marylebone and Belgravia was to provide accommodation for the horses and carriages of the more prosperous of our society of past years and, at the same time, to give lodgings above the stables to the servants who cared for them.

Today, in most Mews one will find the larger stable or garage doors still in use with the restricted but ample residencies above often added to by extensions above the living quarters   The front doors now are more carefully manicured with up-market door furniture and an abundance of potted palms or bay trees outside (most chained to the wall to prevent theft).   Window boxes and large coach lamps often compliment the facades.   Unlike in earlier days these terraced buildings are well maintained and are sought after by those able to afford the exorbitant selling prices.

I was just passing Wimpole Mews when I was hailed by an attractive lady in her late thirties.   She wore her brown hair at shoulder length with a large pair of sunglasses obscuring most of her face.   Her general appearance portrayed a lady of substance; some would suspect one of the *nouveau riche.*

She elegantly entered the cab and in a less than 'cultured' voice asked to be taken to Beak Street on the edge of Soho.

As I mentally prepared my chosen route looking to enter the one-way Beak Street from Lexington Street she asked, "Do you mind if I have a ciggie, I'm dying for a puff?"

"No problem," I replied, "Just keep the windows open if you don't mind."

"Oh thank you," she answered, "I'm visiting some of my old haunts and I'm a bit nervous of who I might bump into so I need some nicotine to keep me going."

"So where does Beak Street feature in your historical travels?"

"Well, I used to work at Murray's Cabaret Club there and got friendly with some guy who was a osteopath. In fact, I lived with him for a while in Wimpole Mews, where you just picked me up, and, through the club and my friend Stephen's mates we got in with some very rich people."

"It was quite exciting for a young girl like me from Uxbridge to get invited to some wild parties at these big houses both in London and outside. I remember going several times to a place called Cliveden somewhere out in Buckinghamshire. There were all these toffs there and I was told that Princess Margaret and other Royals were sometimes there although I never saw them. Anyway, I got to know this Member of Parliament very well and also some Russian guy. I didn't take much notice of who they were or what they did; it was just a whole life of fun to me."

"Then I got involved with this jazz singer called Aloysius, or "Lucky" Gordon, and it all went wrong from then on. Without going into all the details 'Lucky' caused some problems at my house and a gun was fired and the end result was that he was charged with assault and went to prison. That's when the proverbial hit the fan. The police started digging and this MP friend of mine – John somebody or other - was challenged in Parliament that he had had an affair with me. He denied it at first but then admitted it and the whole thing blew up. You see this Russian guy that I knew at Cliveden was thought to be some sort of spy and it was alleged that because my MP was Minister of War or something he was supposed to be a threat to the nation or something and I got dragged in for questioning and everything."

"I suppose this gave 'Lucky' an opportunity to appeal against his imprisonment for my case. In the end, he won his appeal and I got nine months for perjury. I did hear, however, that 'Lucky, later on, got nicked by some young rookie policeman in Soho for having a knife but he got off that as well."

"Then to make matters worse, this osteopath friend of mine got done for living off the immoral earnings of me and my friend. Mandy and me gave evidence at his trial but before the jury decided he went and committed suicide. The whole thing was a complete mess."

"So what did you do after all this?" I asked.

"Well you can imagine I was no longer wanted at these big houses so I gave my story to the tabloids and made a whole wad of money. They were all clambering for my version so I picked the biggest bidder. This was right in the middle of this political carry-on so I suppose that's why they gave us big money. There were also those who wanted to give me 'modelling contracts' so I signed up for one but I said I wouldn't go nude. When the time came the photographer said the producers or somebody said that I agreed in the contract to do nude photos. Anyway, Lewis said he would do some shots with me sitting on a chair looking as if I was nude so that's what we did. He was very sweet about it. The funniest thing about this story is the chair because the one that I sat on was some sort of copy of a famous one and now the both chairs are in the Victoria & Albert Museum."

"Besides the modelling there was also a film, a video, some songs and even a stage show about me and this political affair. Then someone bought a painting that my friend Stephen had done of me some time ago and that went to the National Portrait Gallery. Crazy."

"How do you now feel about this time of your life?" I asked.

"I suppose that I was a bit naïve and got blown away with all the attention. In the end it didn't make me a lot of money – but the lawyers did all right – so afterwards I just kept out of the limelight. I guess that, in the end, I became famous for all the wrong reasons."

"So now I just live quietly alone and do my own thing."

releekenitsirhc

Guess Who Was in My Cab Today

40

I had not long deposited my last fare close to Clapham Common and was driving along the Queenstown Road heading back to central London when I was hailed by a tall portly gentleman who had just left the premises of the Spiritualist Association close to Queen's Circus. He was tall with a ragged handlebar moustache and wearing a winged collar shirt complete with a bowler hat. As he approached I saw that he wore a watch and chain with a Masonic emblem dangling from the central fastener.

"Yes Sir, where can I take you?" I asked.

"Would you take me to Baker Street please, just north of the station" he answered with a very slight Scottish accent, "I have an appointment at 7.30 with a doctor friend who is very punctilious."

As we moved off he volunteered that he also was once a doctor but had taken to writing stories whilst waiting for patients. Entering into conversation with him I said that I thought a doctor's time would be fully occupied leaving little room for anything else.

"Well, you might think that but I had a practice down in Southsea and it was very mundane with few patients. I had been a ship's doctor before that so I suppose I just drifted into working near Portsmouth."

"Do you come from that part of the world?" I enquired.

"No, no I was born in Edinburgh into an Irish family but my father drank too much and that split up the family. We had to move to a tenement flat until a rich uncle came along and paid for me to go to Stonyhurst College and then on to medical school in Edinburgh. I would never have done that if it had not been for him. Whilst in Southsea I specialised in eye problems and needed to get away to London where there was more opportunity. I set up an ophthalmology clinic in Harley Street but that was not too successful either so I concentrated more on writing."

"My first book was called 'A Study in Scarlet' and when I finally found a publisher he paid me a pittance for all the rights and it became a success which made him a lot of money. After that I determined that I would be more bold so when I went to publishers with my next book I asked for much more anticipating that they would refuse but they agreed to pay me what I asked with the result that I became the most well-paid author of my time. I then concentrated more and more on my writing and formed my characters from people that I knew. For example my main character in the series about a detective was based on my old university lecturer and the personality of his side-kick I took from a doctor friend in Portsmouth; other figures I created from my companions at sea."

"Looking back I had quite a time on the south coast. I had always been keen on sport and played football for Portsmouth FA; I was an amateur boxer and in fact was invited to referee a heavyweight championship fight in America but that was just too far to travel. I played golf to a good standard and then I was selected to play cricket for the MCC. I was something of an all rounder but as a bowler I only ever took one first class wicket but it was that of W G Grace so I suppose if you only have one wicket to your name it should be a that of the best batsman of the day." He laughed out loud.

"It was about that time that I became very interested in spiritualism and I went to séances, took part in experiments in telepathy and even got involved in spiritualism missionary work. There was a lot of scepticism of this art at the time and I found myself defending it even though I sometimes had to contend with those who pretended to be with me in my beliefs only to find them afterwards admitting that their paranormal claims had all been a trick. It was very difficult but I guess that I was looking for something to support my beliefs of an after-life. I thought that I might find it in the Masonic movement and I twice joined a lodge but twice resigned. I blame my early life as a catholic for turning me into an atheist. Anyway, I kept up my spiritualism and became a member of the Ghost Club, which is a paranormal investigative and research organisation. When we built the Spiritualism Temple in Camden I was a major contributor to the funds."

"So how did your writing work out?" I queried.

"Oh, that was the main part of my life I suppose. I wrote quite a few novels, over fifty books with my detective character.   In the early days they used to be carried by newspapers and magazines but later on they formed a life of their own.   I know of one very senior Russian policeman who, supposedly, did a doctorate on my detective's life; he must have thought that the stories were true. Quite bizarre. I wrote quite few other books but nothing matched the success of my sleuth and his assistant."

"What was your favourite book?" I asked.

"Strangely, it was one that received less publicity than many of my others. I published it later on in life and it was called 'The Refugees'. It was a story about the Huguenots who were expelled from France in the 18thC by Louise XV and the fate of one family who travelled all the way to North America and the various challenges that they encountered *en route*.   I could, I suppose have based my story in London for large numbers of them came here, particularly, for some reason, to Wandsworth.   In fact there is a road there called Huguenot Place and nearby, in the middle of Trinity Road, is a Huguenot cemetery."

"Well, Sir, here we are in Baker Street. Thank you for such an interesting conversation, it seems that you are in time to meet your friend."   I offered.

"Yes, thank you, cabbie.   My friend, Mycroft, will be impressed and forever grateful to you for getting me here on time.   Goodbye."

elyodnanocruhtraris

Guess Who Was in My Cab Today

41

I had just deposited a family of four at the Lyceum Theatre in Wellington Street, the children proudly holding their tickets for a performance of The Lion King, the long-running musical for the whole family.

As I was about to drive off I was called by a somewhat severe looking man with shoulder-length, neatly combed hair and a winged shirt collar. His suit was dark but a little shabby and my first thought was that he resembled Peter Cook, the satirist and leading left wing comedian. I saw that he held himself carefully aloof with a posture that one often sees on a Shakespearian stage.

As he entered the cab he asked, with a flourish of his hands, to be taken to Charing Cross Road near to Leicester Square where, "I am meeting some fellow thespians for an evening's entertainment" he said.

Having seen that he had came out of the Lyceum I said, " I haven't seen The Lion King but are you somehow involved with the show?"

"Absolutely not," he replied, "but I have long had an association with the Lyceum and in the early days I was the general manager and also actor, director, supervisor of sets and lighting and in charge of casting. In addition I was producing my own stage show of 'The Bells' there so it was a pretty full time involvement."

He then added, "This was a far cry from my roots which were in a working class family in Somerset. I started work at thirteen in a law firm but having seen a production of Hamlet I resolved that my career was to be in the theatre so I took acting lessons and secured some letters of introduction to a theatre in Sunderland. With the help of my cousin, W H Davies who was a poet and author, I secured a position there. You may be familiar with a book my cousin wrote called "The Autobiography of a Super-Tramp'. It was widely published and in later days was a favourite for prescriptive reading in schools."

"However, it was my production of the play 'The Bells' by Leopold Lewis which brought me to notice for I was playing 'Mathias', the leading part, and it gained enormous revues which brought us to London. On the opening night here I again played the leading man and was very pleased with the way that the show went but my wife, who had been in the audience and was pregnant with our second son, was not so impressed and in our carriage on the way home said to me, 'Are you going to go on making a fool of yourself like this all your life?'. That was just too much so I stopped the carriage at Hyde Park Corner and got out and walked off into the night never to see her again."

"We didn't divorce but when many years later I was knighted she had the temerity to insist on being known as Lady Florence. She probably clung on to that 'position' partly because I was the first actor to be so honoured. Although I had had little to do with my two children they did follow me into the theatre but my youngest son and his wife died in a maritime disaster aboard the Empress of Ireland liner off of Canada when it was in collision with a Norwegian ship. My eldest son went on to become a noted actor and dramatist."

"It wasn't always an easy life as an actor; I remember once getting stage fright and being hissed off of the stage but by and large I must say that things improved, certainly whilst I was playing Mathias, at the Lyceum. The theatre was resurrected as a leading venue and it prospered from my management. I began to stage Shakespearian plays and brought in an American actress named Ellen Terry. She took the leading female roll to my male lead and we developed a close working relationship. I also had a very good partnership with Bram Stoker who, you may remember, created 'Dracula'. He was my business manager there during the successful times."

"I have played at all of the major theatres in London and in the provinces and have met a great number of leading players."

"There was, however, one disturbing episode in my thespian days when I received a death threat from a fellow artist. His name was Richard Prince and he had been committed to Broadmoor for murdering another actor at, would you believe, the stage door of the Adelphi Theatre. It seemed that he took umbrage at my criticism of the lenient sentence on him. I remember commenting that Prince would never be executed because his victim was an actor! Anyhow, he somewhere got hold of my address and threatened that he would kill me when he was released. Nothing came of it co course and I went on to received a number of honorary degrees from universities here and abroad and other sorts of honours and medals."

"So what now of the future?" I asked.

"Oh! I have played a number of leading roles in my life so there is nothing now that I crave. I suppose we all aspire to end our days in glory and for me that would be to die in harness; to die on stage whilst delivering the final soliloquy of a great and gifted character. "

"In addition, because we actors, by virtue of our calling, are generally quite egotistic and narcissistic I would welcome the erection of a statue in my honour in the middle of London's theatre-land. That would be marvellous and fitting."

As I set him down outside of the National Portrait Gallery he paid the fare, with a generous tip, and strode off in a manner presenting an impression that he owned that part of the West End and was ready to welcome any recognition that might be forthcoming.

gnivriyrnehris

Guess Who Was in My Cab Today

42

The imposing façade of the National Gallery with its eight columns supporting the portico gazes out from the north side of Trafalgar Square with an air of ownership and superiority.   Originally conceived in 1824 The National Gallery began life across the Square in Carlton House Terrace with a collection of thirty-eight paintings bought from the Angerstein estate. Today, this publicly owned treasure houses over 2000 pieces of art including works by Constable, Raphael, Turner and Titian and is the fourth most visited museum in the world.

As I waited at the pedestrian traffic lights at Pall Mall East about to enter the west side of the Square I saw coming towards me a man in a paint spattered smock with long flowing hair and an equally long beard.   A ragged hat covered a rugged face and domed head and his right hand was in a sling.   His left hand was holding a clutch of notebooks, which were secured to his belt by a cord.

"Yes, sir", I greeted him as he entered the cab, "Where can I take you?"

"Pleeze to the British Library" he said in a distinct Italian accent "I have to look at some drawings there while I am in London."

"Are you just on a short visit admiring our works of art?" I asked.

"Yes, it is very nice," he replied, "but I have come to discuss an exhibition of fifteen of my own paintings and drawings that the National Gallery is putting on shortly."

"That is amazing," I ventured, "So you are an artist and obviously of some repute."

"Yes, I studied at the studio of Verrocchio in Florence for several years as his apprentice before he allowed me to contribute to one of his paintings 'Christ with John the Baptist'; he permitted me to paint the angel holding Christ's robe.   That was a great honour for me, an uneducated and illegitimate boy from the country."

"My mother was a poor peasant girl and my father a nobleman. My education was very basic but the Tuscan countryside became my schoolroom. I filled hundreds of notebooks with drawings of plants, animals and flora often in minute detail. At thirteen I decided that I wanted to paint and the only place for that was in Florence which was a magnet for young artists. With Verrocchio I learned to sculpture and work in stone and bronze, I studied architecture, anatomy, music, engineering and botany. More importantly I immersed myself in drawing and painting."

"When I set up my own studio I was able to work to commissions of portraits by wealthy merchants but it also gave me access to other fields or interest. I was allowed by the civic authorities to go to the mortuaries and dissect human cadavers and carefully record in drawings the details of the muscles and tendons of the human body. I did this by carefully drawing back the skin to reveal the under body. I also made detailed sketches of the other organs like the heart, the lungs and the kidneys."

"After a problem with the criminal authorities in Florence which involved my own apprentice, Salai, I went to Milan which was a wealthy and ostentatious city. I attended a gathering at the court of the Duke of Milan, and I went as a musician with a solid silver violin in the shape of a horse's head but I was really there to gain his employment not as an artist but as an inventor. I showed him drawings that I had made of weapons of war, of a double hull boat, of a flying machine and of how to test the tensions of wire. This interested him a lot as he was always under threat from neighbouring states. He could not understand my introductory letter or CV because it was in mirror writing, that is because I am left-handed I always wrote from right to left so you needed a mirror to read." He gave a gleeful chuckle at the memory.

"I was always looking out for interesting things to draw" he went on, "If I saw a particularly striking face in the crowd, for example, I would follow that man or woman until I had sketched the outline sufficiently to make a full drawing later on. Actually, there is such a face in my fresco of The Last Supper which I was asked to paint in a convent in Milan. I call it a fresco but in fact it was not true fresco for I used a different method of painting which was a disaster. Instead of painting quickly on to moist plaster, a true fresco, I used a new style of painting with oils on to an already dried plaster.

Consequently, it did not retain its colour or its composition and after a while it began to flake."

"The face of Peter was taken from a sketch that is in one of my notebooks.   It was not an attractive profile but, to me, portrayed the rugged, argumentative nature of Peter.   It is not so apparent in the original Last Supper but I believe that there is a copy of my 'fresco' here in England at the Royal Academy of Arts.   This was done by one of my disciples a few years after my original and his depiction of Peter is better than mine."

"After this convent commission, some clients began to claim that I was unreliable.   This may have started during my painting of The Last Supper because the Prior of the Convent did not understand why I would paint from dawn 'til dusk even without stopping to eat but then rest for three or four days.   Sometimes I found it difficult to finish a portrait or other commission.   Often, there was very little more to do to complete the task but I suppose that I became tired of the subject or was distracted by other things.   Also, those who commissioned me were frequently very demanding and hard to satisfy."

"There was one portrait that I was asked to do by a nobleman named *del Giocondo*. He wanted a portrait of his wife but was dissatisfied at every stage with what I was producing. She was quite ugly and because I tried to make her more attractive he kept arguing that it was not a true portrait.   So in the end I just painted her as she was. He was satisfied, his wife, Lisa, was happy and they paid me even though there were some minor unfinished parts but they were unaware of this.   I then went back to my studio and painted my own version of her as a beautiful and enigmatic lady and it is this version that subsequently attracted much attention and is now in the Louvre."

"So, are there any surprises in the forthcoming exhibition?" I asked.

"Well, I am given to understand that one of my least known paintings is coming over from America.   It is called the Salvata Mundi and was painted for the King of France where I had spent a lot of time; but we shall see if it does in fact feature in the exhibition."

As we arrived at the British Library I saw that he had been sketching in his tethered notebook.   I could not quite see just what he was drawing only that the face had a very bushy moustache and heavy eyebrows and he was copying the reflection from my rear-view mirror.

He was clearly a man of phenomenal intellect and talent.

icnivadodranoel

Guess Who Was in My Cab Today

43

My previous fare was a family of three young children with an elderly man and woman whom I had dropped off at the Odeon Cinema at Marble Arch. The children were excited because they were about to see the film, *Harry Potter and the Philosopher's Stone*; clearly a treat from their doting grandparents.

It is always a bonus for a cab driver when he can pick up a fare immediately after dropping off another. I saw this gentleman before he saw me but on doing so he waved for me to wait. At first I thought that he might have just emerged from an Aladdin pantomime for he was a big man with extraordinary long bushy eyebrows that drooped either side of his face. Beneath the eyebrows was a neatly combed and full beard that fell below his collar line and settled on his chest. Above was a pulled back topknot of hair. He wore long flowing and somewhat exotic robes with very wide sleeves. On the enormous cuffs were some Chinese letters with ornate decorations.

On reaching the driver's door he asked in quite clear but accented Oriental tones if I could take him to the Chinese Quarter. I queried if the Wardour Street end of Gerrard Street was OK for him. He said that he wanted to visit the place where the Chinese New Year was celebrated so I confirmed that my suggestion was right in the centre of Chinatown and Gerrard Street was exactly where the celebrations took place.

As we turned off towards Park Lane he was absorbing everything he saw with a look of incredulity on his face and volunteered that things in London were very different from where he originated in China. "I come from the remote district of Tsow in north-eastern China where my father had been a soldier and then became Governor of the region," he said. "My father's first marriage produced nine girls and desirous of a son he had, when in his seventies, married the daughter of one of his friends. The product of that marriage was me, the son that he wanted so much. I was born in a cave to my father's second wife but he died when I was three years old so was brought up by my mother in some poverty."

"My schooling was in the ancient Six Arts comprising music, archery, charioteering, rites, calligraphy and mathematics but it was not until I was fifteen that I decided to turn my mind to learning."

"And how did you progress from there?" I asked.

"At nineteen I married a girl from a neighbouring province and, to support my family, I gained employment by the state as keeper of the stores of grain and then in charge of public fields and lands. I became a teacher and earned the respect of my students whom I didn't charge for my services. My philosophy was that I would not deprive an avid learner of advancing himself because he could not afford to be taught and I never turned away a student despite of or because of their wealth. Having said that, I would not refuse a symbolic gift of a meal or similar from those who could afford to do so. I came to the notice of the Duke of the area who saw that I was teaching young men in the doctrines of antiquity and, with his patronage, I progressed from there".

"I suppose that my teachings were philosophical in nature for I promoted personal and governmental morality and correctness in social relationships, justice and sincerity. I believed in strong family loyalty, and respect of the elders. I loved my work and I often cited to my students the maxim, '*Choose a job you like and you will never work a day in your life*'. In fact, many times I used maxims as a way of conveying ethics and pure living in my teachings."

"You see, many of my students were from the poorer regions and, like me, had received limited early tuition. Whilst I could see that they had an in-depth morality in their lives they needed to be able concisely to sum up those principles in short one-line statements. Hence, my teachings were in simple statements that encompassed all that needed to be said.'"

"Another of my maxims was, '*The man who chases two rabbits catches neither*' and was an indications to them that they should concentrate on one goal at a time."

"I encouraged them to question everything telling them that '*The man who asks a question is a fool for a minute; the man who does not ask is a fool for life*' and in emphasising this I advised, '*He who knows all the answers has not asked all the questions.*'"

"I preached that morality in life is of paramount importance and I would underline this by advocating that '*What you do not wish for yourselves you do not do unto others*'. Equally, and one of my favourites, was '*Before you embark on a journey of revenge, dig two graves*'."

"Some tried to say that because I used terms like 'heaven' and 'the afterlife' I was preaching a religious dimension but I never moved into spiritual thinking such as the nature of souls which is considered essential to religious thought and the Catholic Jesuits, who were the first to translate my works, publicly declared that my teachings were not idolatry but more akin to the Chinese interpretation of humanism."

As we approached Wardour Street I could not stop myself from asking if he could give me one last quote of advice. He laughed and thought for a moment and then said, "Well, from myself I would say that '*Our greatest glory is not in never falling but in rising every time we fall*'".

"However, and, sadly, this is not from me but from a wise counsellor who came later although I wish I had thought of it first. It is '*Learn today as if you will live forever but live today as if you will die tomorrow*'".

With that he paid his fare and disappeared among many of his fellow citizens into the throngs of Gerrard Street.

suicufnoc

Guess Who Was in My Cab Today

44

Temporarily halted in traffic on the City Road in Islington I was admiring the Georgian architecture of Wesley's Chapel, the origin of which is now over two hundred years old, when a lady in her senior years emerged from the cobbled courtyard and signalled to me to pull in. She was smartly dressed in a blue two-piece suit sporting a distinct single row of pearls. Her hair was coiffured and she carried, what to me appeared to be, a very expensive handbag.

As she climbed into the cab she asked in a clipped but very well spoken voice for me to take her to the Ritz Hotel in Piccadilly. She was alone and appeared to be a little pre-occupied as if reflecting on something that was taking all of her attention.

I don't often open the conversation with a fare but in this case I gauged that she might just want to off-load her thoughts so I gently asked if she had found the Wesley Museum interesting.

"Oh." She said, as if I had brought her back to herself, "No. I wasn't at the Museum but just went in to see if the gift that my husband and I gave to the chapel all those years ago was still there and in use."

"You see, my husband and I were married there many years ago and now that my husband had passed on I like to visit various places and remember our days together."

"I was brought up as a strict Wesleyan Methodist by my father who owned two grocery shops but was also a Methodist local preacher so it was right that I should marry in a Wesleyan chapel.   Later in our married life we donated money to this chapel for a Communion Rail to be erected partly in his memory but also to give thanks for our marriage.   I am pleased to see that the Rail is still there.   I have a lot to be thankful for in my life, my husband was a very successful business-man and had made his fortune before we met."

"I had left Grammar School in Lincolnshire and was fortunate to get a scholarship to study chemistry at Oxford.   Whilst there I had become interested in politics and joined the Oxford University Conservative

Association subsequently becoming its President. My husband later offered to finance another degree in law and politics which set me on a career as a Member of Parliament."

"At some point it was suggested that my somewhat shrill voice could be a disadvantage so I was persuaded to take voice lessons with none other than Laurence Olivier. I cannot remember if that was before or after I was selected as the Conservative candidate for Finchley but from then on I never really looked back. Once in Parliament I soon became a member of the Front Bench as Under-secretary in the Ministry of Pensions and National Insurance and then a Shadow member when we were in opposition to Labour. When we regained power under Ted Heath I became a member of the Cabinet as Secretary of State for Education. "

"Subsequently, Ted Heath lost two general elections in the same year so there were moves afoot to replace him as leader. I stood against him, for which he never forgave me, and became the Leader of the Opposition and, later, the first woman Prime Minister. It was not, however, without its trials and tribulations. I had inherited the IRA problem in Northern Ireland where too, too many of our wonderful soldiers and policemen were being murdered by the cowardly terrorists. There were also many violent demonstrations against The National Front; the deployment of Cruise Missiles at Greenham Common, and later the Miners Strikes and the introduction of the Poll Tax."

"The biggest problem, however, was the invasion of The Falkland Islands by the Argentinians. This was a deliberate attempt by one country to aggressively seize land from another in the face of International Law. We had little option but to immediately send in our troops to free our British people living there. Our military carried out a magnificent operation thousands of miles away in recapturing our islands within two months. Sadly, we lost over two hundred brave young men in the conflict. When I visited The Falklands later I toured in the Governor's maroon taxicab just like this. I have no idea how a London taxi ended up so far away."

"Perhaps the brightest period of my time as Prime Minister was when I met with and established a brilliant working relationship with Mikhail Gorbachev. The Cold War had always been a cloud hanging over International relationships but with Gorbachev I sensed that we could do business and there is no doubt that it was his leadership of the Soviet Republic at that particular time that was the beginning of the end of the Cold War and the break-up of the Soviet Union. He was a truly remarkable man."

"Equally, the saddest time was when some very good friends of mine were killed and injured by the IRA's attempt to murder the British Cabinet with their bomb in Brighton. We were there for the annual Conservative Conference and after the attack many wanted me to cancel my concluding address but that would have handed success to these murderers. I made the speech albeit with some minor amendments to show that their evil actions would never succeed."

"May I ask you", I interjected, "why you did not persist with the Poll Tax which, to me, was eminently sensible in spreading local community costs among all those who used the services rather than just the named house-holder?"

"Well, of course I did persist with the change and it was my successor as Prime Minister who relented and scrapped the Poll Tax. That may have been in light of that major demonstration in Trafalgar Square a few months before, only he can say. For my part, when I made a decision nothing would turn me back from that. I have always been resolute in seeing through any decision that I made. I think that it was the Soviets who gave me the nickname, '*The Iron Lady*' which I think is quite appropriate, one always has to be resolute, it is in one's nature."

As I set this remarkable lady down at the door of the Ritz I could not help but think that her statue in the Members' Lobby of the House of Commons would have been more apt had it been made not of bronze but of iron.

rehctchtteragram

Guess Who Was in My Cab Today

45

Leicester Square is a small grassy enclave situated in the heart of theatre land that has now almost lost its identity as a specific location to the surrounding area by which most people now know it.

The square itself dates from the 17thC and originally was a collection of fields around a newly built Leicester House.   In time the area became loosely residential, then an area of entertainment boasting some major theatres nearby and latterly a focal place for cinemagoers and the street entertainer.

Leicester Square attracts all types of people from the theatre aficionado to the travelling busker; from the homeless to the hustler; from the mundane to the outlandish and so it was no real surprise, as I waited on the nearby rank, to be approached by a somewhat plump man in his late forties with a balding head and hair falling each side over his ears. He had a goatee beard and moustache and was wearing a brown leather jerkin with a narrow starched white collar and what looked like a university gown over his shoulders. He carried a leather satchel and tucked behind his right ear was a quill.

"Yes, sir" I greeted him as he drew near, "where can I take you?"

"My dear sir," he responded, whilst theatrically waving his arms around, "please take me to the Globe Theatre just over the river from St Paul's, I have some business there."

As he got into the cab I saw that the fingers of his right hand were heavily stained black with what may have been ink.   There were also specks of black on his white collar and around his mouth.

We moved off towards Charing Cross Road heading for the Strand and I could see him muttering to himself as if rehearsing some speech or address.   I was somewhat reluctant to disturb his train of thought but I really did wish to know more about this man.   Therefore, with somewhat bated breath I said, "Fine old theatre, the Globe.   I understand that it was burnt down at some point."

"Yes, indeed, " he said, "There was a cannon being used in the play Henry VIII, and it misfired and set light to the roof thatching and wooden beams."

"How unfortunate," I responded, "was anyone hurt?"

"Sadly yes, one stagehand whose trousers caught fire when the thatch fell. He had to be extinguished by people throwing beer over him." He giggled at the thought.   "I shouldn't laugh," he continued, "that theatre meant much to me and, as a play-wright, it deprived me of an important venue at which to perform my work.   This all happened just as we were recovering from another bout of the bubonic plague where, for some seven years or so, we were constantly opening and closing as the epidemic swirled around us."

"My whole life has been given over to my first true love, writing and to acting when I could, so to have our theatres closed meant no acting work and very few opportunities to sell or stage my plays."

"So what sort of plays do you write?" I asked.

"Well, I switch between comedies, tragedies and the historical.   Most are generally well received but it is a foregone conclusion that some will criticise them and try to undermine my work.   That is where my wife Anne, is very good, she has a level head and, I suppose, being eight years older than me, she can easier dismiss theses critics.   I should not be so sensitive for I have lived through some tough times especially when my mother, who was from a pious Catholic family, was in fear of her life during the persecution of those practising their faith.   I never followed her choice of religion, no, I embraced the official Church of England ministry both in marriage and in the baptism of my children."

"But you asked about my plays.   I have written 39 plays and any number of sonnets.   I like to write scenarios where I can alternate between the light-hearted and the serious and I enjoy acting in my plays – and in other people's.   I have had quite a number of roles, particularly at the Globe where I once played a ghost in one of my own productions so I suppose, in truth, I am equally at home as an actor or as a dramatist."

"The sad thing is that there are any number of jealous followers of our art who seek to make mischief by claiming that the writings were by someone else other than the playwright. They have done that to me by whispering abroad that my work was not mine at all but by Christopher Marlowe or Francis Bacon or some other writer. It has never been a secret in our trade that most playwrights collaborate with others in the production of their works. Just because I help another with an idea or a proposed route for a plot in no way would I ever seek to claim authorship."

"So what of the future?" I asked him.

"Oh!, I was conceived and nurtured in Stratford-upon-Avon where my father was a successful glove maker and my mother part of a land-owning farming family. I live between there, where my wife has a cottage, and London so I guess that Stratford is where I shall retire when my writing days are over. For the present I am in perfect health."

He suddenly pulled a sketch-pad out of his bag as if he had just remembered something and said, "Excuse me, dear driver, but do you perchance have a soft leaded pencil? I have a need to quickly make a sketch for my next play whilst I remember so a grade 2B, if you have one, would be perfect."

"But as for the future," he mused, "the important thing for me is that wherever I am laid to rest there I must remain. I have already left strict instructions in my Will that, once buried, I am never to be moved and, just to make sure, carved on my tombstone will be the epitaph, *'then cursed be he who moves my bones'.*"

eraepsekahsmailliw

Guess Who Was in My Cab Today

46

I had just dropped off four young members of the Blues & Royals Regiment at the Knightsbridge Barracks in Hyde Park and was heading back along the relatively quiet South Carriage Drive towards Mayfair.

As I approached Albert Gate I reflected on how this was once a bridge crossing the Westbourne River which ran along the south side of the Park. It is said that the name, 'Knightsbridge' by which the area is known, derives from a duel between two knights who, supposedly, once fought to the death on this bridge. Certainly, Hyde Park was well known as a 'duelling spot' even as late as the 18th C.

In 1730 the Westbourne River was dammed to create the Serpentine and the two Inns that stood either side of the Albert Gate were demolished and replaced by Thomas Cubitt buildings. The one to the east of the Gate became the French Embassy and remains so to this day.

On passing the rear entrance of the Embassy on south Carriage Drive I saw a very tall man, some 6 feet 5 inches in height, who appeared to be looking for a cab. As I slowed he beckoned to me to stop and crossed over the road and asked in a strong Gallic accent to be taken to Carlton Gardens. If one were ever to generalise about the looks of any particular nationality then I could be forgiven for instantly recognising the French features. He had a long square face with a similarly long nose and slanted eyes. His ears were quite prominent and he sported a rather small moustache that was about the width of his upper lip. In confirmation of my surmise he was dressed in French military uniform complete with an ornately decorated kepi.

Once he had settled himself I asked, "Whereabouts in Carlton Gardens would you like?"

He replied, "I would like number 4 please," and reflected, "It was my headquarters in London many years ago. You see, my country was invaded by an Italian/German alliance and our government decided to cooperate with the invaders but I could not be part of that. I had been a military man all of my life. I fought in the First World War on the Front Line and was injured three times. I was then captured and held prisoner for almost three years and tried five times to escape, once in a laundry basket and another by digging a tunnel. My last attempt was by trying to impersonate a nurse but my height gave me away: He giggled at the thought.

"After the War I sought a secondment to the War College but, at first, I was refused because it seems that I was in the habit of upsetting people.   They said that I was arrogant." (He sniffed at the suggestion.)

"At the beginning of the Second World War, as a colonel, I had command of a tank division and we had several skirmishes with the Germans. I had the ear of some government ministers and often sat in on high-level war meetings. Later, when I was promoted to brigadier general, I was invited to become the under-secretary for war.   Before my country's capitulation I made frequent trips to London to discuss our position with British and American leaders."

"Once the French government had given in I flew to London to set up a government in exile with the Free French Forces and urged all French people to resist the occupation.   Three times every month I broadcast to the French people.   My relations with the UK and USA leaders were not good and I know that Churchill wanted me dismissed as the leader of the Free French.   I argued that far from that I should be regarded as leader of France."

"The collaborating French Vichy government distanced themselves from me and at one point they convicted me *in absentia* and sentenced me to death but I knew that my broadcasts were uniting the French people and I was popular among the French soldiers."

"The British and the Americans did not treat us a real allies; they never consulted us and used the French forces for their own goals. Our relationship with the leaders of the Allies was, shall we say, fractured.   Churchill's wife once said to me, "General, you must not hate your friends more than you hate your enemies" I told her, 'No nation has friends, only interests'."

"There was also an incident in Britain - I cannot say for what reason or with whom responsibility lay - but there was an assassination attempt on my life when an aeroplane taking me to Scotland to address the Free French Navy was sabotaged. Fortunately, my pilot landed safely."

"And so in the end the Germans were pushed back and we gradually recaptured France. The British did not see the liberation of Paris as a priority and were prepared to allow the French Communists to take the lead but I would not have that and it was I who made the grand entrance into Paris as the liberator. I was shot at whilst leading my officers along the Place de Concorde and even as I walked down the aisle of the Notre Dame I was again fired upon. But they shoot like pigs."

"After the War I became President but France was in a bad shape. There was huge destruction, disease, destroyed crops and the black market; so there was much to do. In addition, I had to deal with the communists in my government. On the political scene there were efforts for me to sign the Nuclear Power Test Ban Treaty but I supported the idea of France becoming a nuclear power so I refused to sign."

"I had resigned as President over a domestic issue and whilst I was absent France had agreed the setting up of the European Economic Community or the Common Market as the British called it. When I again became President I had to resist what some of the EEC members were pushing for which was a move towards some form of political integration. I objected for that, in my mind, would impinge upon the sovereignty of France."

"The British did not at first want to join the EEC and chose instead to remain in the European Free Trade Area. When afterwards they thought that they would join I said "No" because the French standards had began to exceed those of Britain and the EEC was a stronger trade block than the EFTA. The Americans tried to change my mind to allow Britain to join but I was always conscious that Churchill once said that if he had to choose between France and the United States he would choose the USA so I said "No" again and again."

"When I eventually retired for good I wrote my memoirs and spent time with my family, especially my beautiful daughter, Anne, who had Down syndrome."

"So why", I asked "Did you take such a dislike to Britain after all that they had done for France in the war?" He sniffed again, paid his fare and left muttering "Non, Non, Non" as he walked away.

elluagedselrahclareneg

Guess Who Was in My Cab Today

47

Sometimes, the City of London can be quite claustrophobic with its myriad of road junctions, traffic lights, one-way streets, jaywalking pedestrians and cyclists that consider themselves invincible. On one such day I decided that I would feel much more comfortable in the environs of the West End and had left the Bank junction heading down Queen Victoria Street.

As I breathed out a sigh of relief in satisfaction of leaving the Square Mile I caught sight of a uniformed man beckoning me to stop. He was gently holding the elbow of an elderly man who was carrying a white stick. This man was tall with a very large white beard and wearing what appeared to be a Victorian jacket and waistcoat, a white bow tie and a rather battered Homburg hat.

As I drew to a stop, the 'uniform' said, "Could you take this gentleman to Denmark Hill in Camberwell please, he needs to be there for a meeting at three o'clock". He carefully settled the old man into the cab and bade him goodbye.

Quickly deciding that I was fortunate to have an easy route over Blackfriars Bridge, through the Elephant & Castle and down the Walworth Road I immediately tuned almost into autopilot thankful to be heading out of the centre of London to quieter streets.

I looked in my rear-view mirror and saw the serene facial features of my passenger aware, of course, that he probably could not see me at all. As we crossed Blackfriars Bridge I said to him, "That was very kind of the commissionaire to get you a cab."

He replied, "Oh that was not a commissionaire, he is one of our officers in our headquarters there in Queen Victoria Street. Simon had been with us for many years and he has served in France, Sweden, New Zealand and also Canada. He has been a loyal member of our ministry and a dedicated servant to all those people that need help wherever they are. Now he has charge of the soup kitchens that we run; he is very good at organising."

"You see, I came from a privileged background, at least until I was about twelve but my father's fortunes took a downward turn and I was withdrawn from my school because he no longer could afford the fees. I was apprenticed to a pawnbroker and, I suppose, over the three of four years that I was there I saw a lot of heartache and real poverty with mothers, often with drunken husbands, pawning their essential articles to buy a little time and money to feed their children. I had become a Methodist and was a preacher evangelising in the poorer areas of Nottingham against their plight and drunkenness and the moral failures of our society."

"When I could not find employment there I came to London and again worked in a pawnbrokers where I found exactly the same conditions for the poor. I was not sure that the Methodist Church was doing that which I thought necessary so I formed the Methodist Reform Society and went out preaching in the public places, often near public houses, extolling the virtues of following the Gospels, repentance, sobriety and helping the poor. When the Methodists banned me from campaigning I became independent and formed the Christian Revival Society that then became the East London Christian Mission. It was then that we started the 'Soup Kitchen'."

"My eldest son worked with us and once when I referred to us as volunteers he said that he was not a volunteer, he was a regular so that really was the catalyst for us aligning ourselves to the military in our uniforms, our music and with our own flag. We became the Salvation Army, I was the General and our helpers became officers. We adopted local folklore songs and put our own Christian words to the music which we sang outside pubs."

"We faced a lot of opposition from the alcohol selling industry who feared a loss of revenue if we managed to persuade the poor to give up drinking. Gangs would disrupt our marches and meetings and they would assault our soldiers. The Press vilified us by mocking our motto of 'Blood and Fire' saying it related to the blood of sinners and the fire of hell. In fact, it was simply the Blood of Christ and the Fire of the Holy Spirit. They also claimed that I was a charlatan seeking to make money. Even the Church of England described me as the Anti-Christ but nobody could ever question my compassion for the most needy of society."

"I know that some found my methods somewhat dictatorial, even some of my own family were critical and I know that I was hard to work with and demanded absolute commitment but the poor people who had been led astray needed and deserved our help. I used to travel the country on our motor-cade preaching the need to turn away from vice, to create shelter for the homeless, the emigrants and 'fallen women' and help for the drunkards and released prisoners. It was a hard journey but eventually our fortunes changed and our mission was recognised by the great and the good. Royalty welcomed me; I was given an honorary degree by Oxford University, the Freedom of the City of London and even invited to the King's Coronation. We established the Army in as many as fifty-eight different countries including the United States. I visited each of them to hold Salvation Meetings. We regularly published a magazine and I wrote several books, one of which became a best seller in which I set out a modern welfare approach to society's ills. My philosophy was that it is the duty of each Christian to step into the breach."

"Today we still produce booklets and ecumenical documents but we also have charity shops and the public still expect to see us singing Carols in the shopping arcades at Christmas. We continue to work with the homeless and others who are the unfortunates in our society and, thankfully, we still have need of our Training Centre in Champion Hill."

"And what," I asked, "about your mobile Tea Wagon? I remember seeing it at major emergencies in London, in fact they were often the first of the support services to arrive."

"Yes," he answered. " It is important when engaged in our usual work not to forget the emergency services at times of crisis or public disorder. They have need not only of cups of tea but also of pastoral care when they have been involved in some nasty situations. I see that also as part of our role."

As we approached the Training Centre I asked him how he would like to be remembered.

"Oh! A rose named after me or perhaps even a steam locomotive; I don't suppose there will ever be a beer dedicated to me," he said with a wry smile. With that another of his 'uniformed officers' came out, paid his fare and escorted him into the Salvation Army edifice.

htoobmailliw

Guess Who Was in My Cab Today

48

The Old Kent Road is not a normal hunting ground for cabbies although it is often used by them as a main thoroughfare when on a long trip to or from the suburbs of south London. Such was the case when I was making my way back to central London from a trip 'down south'.

I was travelling along that major artery back into town and found myself passing the iconic *Thomas A Beckett* public house at the junction with Albany Road. For those with a sporting interest the pub will automatically be recognised for its upstairs gymnasium where many famous boxers have, over the years, used it a training camp prior to their world championship fights.

It had long passed its prime at this point but I was intrigued when a tall, black man, smartly dressed and with an air of confidence came skipping out of the front door and waved to me to stop. As he came alongside my cab I saw that he had clearly been a handsome man in his youth and still portrayed a distinguished and upright bearing. I noticed that his hands were perceptibly shaking and his voice had more of a southern American drawl which could easily have been mistaken for a slur to his speech.

"Yes, Sir" I greeted him, "where can I take you?"

"Good day to you" he responded. "I would like to go to the Arsenal stadium please, I am on a journey of memories whilst here in London. I have already been to Wembley Arena and I have one ore two other points to visit before I return home to Louiseville in Kentucky."

As I headed off towards London Bridge he settled himself in the back of the cab and proceeded to reminisce out loud of his last visits to the Thomas A Beckett some years ago.

"I take it that you are in the boxing game" I suggested.

"Yes," he said, "I have been a boxer all of my life and when I fought in London this, as with many professional boxers, was my main training camp. It has a long history for our sport so there really was no question of going anywhere else."

"So how did you get into what some regard as a barbaric sport?"

"Oh" he replied, "I was brought up in downtown Louiseville where life was pretty tough. There was a lot of prejudice against us black people and there was not much future for the likes of me, especially as I now know that I was also dyslexic. You know that once I was even refused a glass of water because of my colour. Strangely, it was a Kentucky cop who started me on this boxing road. I was about twelve and I was going to whelp another boy who stole my bike and this cop grabbed me and said, "Son, if you're going to do that you had better first learn to fight". So I joined this amateur boxing club and did quite well. In fact, I won quite a few amateur bouts and I made the Olympic boxing team. Then at the age of eighteen I won the gold medal at the Rome Olympics as a light-heavyweight and became professional that same year."

"Since then I have never looked back. There was no way that I was going to be trapped in my black heritage that came from my ancestors being slaves. Shortly after a few professional fights I joined the Nation of Muslim and changed my name. I was world heavyweight champion within four years and had won nineteen fights, fifteen by a knockout. Then the trouble began. I was called up for conscription into the US military and told that I was going to war in Vietnam. I refused because of my religious beliefs. I was arrested and fined and stripped of my boxing licence and titles and it was nearly four years before the Supreme Court quashed my conviction and I could fight again."

"I had lost four years of my prime time as a fighter and when I got back I needed to tell people just how good I was. When I fought Sonny Liston I told him that he was a 'the big ugly bear' and said that 'after I had beaten him I would donate him to a zoo'. They tried to blind me in the fight by putting something on his gloves and rubbing it into my eyes but I got through that and I won by a technical knock-out when he failed to come out of his corner for the seventh round. It was then that I stood up on the ropes and told the world, "I am the greatest" and " I was the prettiest thing that ever lived. " That has stayed with me."

"I twice beat your Henry Cooper and the first time at Wembley Arena he did floor me but I cut him badly below the eye and the referee stopped the fight.   The second time at the Arsenal Stadium I again cut his eye and the fight was stopped again."

"When I fought Joe Frazier I wound him up by telling him that he was 'too dumb to be champion' and by calling him 'Uncle Tom'.   With George Foreman it was easy to get him riled.   I told him during the fight that I had prepared by wrestling with an alligator and handcuffing lightning and that I was so mean that I made medicine sick.   I must say that George Foreman was the greatest fighter of all time – next to me."   He laughed at the memory of his joke.

"I used to enjoy speaking to the press in language that they could afterwards quote of me.   They seemed to have enjoyed my 'Float like a butterfly, sting like a bee' and often used it in their newspaper reports.   I remember that when I was assessed for the military the authorities had great pleasure in downgrading my academic ability from 1A to 1Y because of my dyslexia.   I told them that `I said I was the greatest not the smartest'."

"After the twin-towers terrorist attacks on September 11th many white Americans started saying that Islam was a hate religion with a leaning towards violence.   I was asked for my views and I told the press that those who carried out the attack were not true Muslims."

I asked him, "Apart from your sporting achievements how would you like to be remembered?"

"Well," he drawled, "I suppose that the things that I used to say in a sort of rhyming way I was really the first 'Rapper'.   That would be good.   I just wish that people would love everybody else the way that they all love me.   It would be a better world."

He paid his fare and took a step further along his memory lane.

iladernmahom

Guess Who Was in My Cab Today

49

Hamilton Square in Bermondsey houses a small block of what were tenement style flats a stone's throw from the back of Guy's Hospital. I had just dropped off a nurse at the hospital when I was waved at by a tall gentleman in naval uniform wearing a bicorn hat and sporting a cutlass or sword in a brass and leather sheath. His bushy grey hair stood out over his ears and I noticed that he appeared blind in his right eye.

He climbed into the cab a little gingerly and I saw that the right sleeve of his tunic was empty and the cuff was fastened across his breast. He had clearly suffered much.

"Yes Sir" I greeted him where can I take you?"

In a slight Norfolk accent he said, "I would like to go to the top of The Mall, to the Admiralty building please."

As we set off I saw in the rear view mirror that he was securing the buttons on his waistcoat with his left hand. He was surprisingly adept at managing with just one hand for so difficult a task. I said to him, "Not wishing to upset you, sir, but I am amazed at how you manage so well with one arm."

"Well driver," he answered, "I have been in the wars somewhat. You see I lost the sight in my right eye in Corsica at the siege of Calvi. I was commanding *HMS Agamemnon* and we were supporting the Corsicans in trying to dislodge the French from their garrison there. I received a musket bullet to my eye and eventually went blind. So that was the first injury of any seriousness."

"My arm was lost at the battle of Santa Cruz in Tenerife. We had been advised that Spanish treasure convoys were regularly bringing their loads from the Americas into the harbour there and the Admiral charged me with mounting an attack from my ship, *HMS Theseus,* to seize the city. Things didn't quite go according to plan and our attack during darkness was discovered and the Spaniards started firing on us that prevented us from getting our ships close to the shore. I took my men in sloops with muffled oars but I was hit in my right arm by grapeshot and had to be taken back to my flagship. The surgeon couldn't save it and so it was amputated. He ignored my request to let me keep my arm and threw it into the sea."

"We had managed to land over a thousand men into the port but we could not take the garrison. My men were trapped; they could not leave and no support could go to their rescue so we had to negotiate a withdrawal. Eventually we secured a truce with the Spanish general and our men were allowed to retreat with full military honours and we agreed not to burn their town. In gratitude for the general's compassion I sent him a letter along with some British beer and cheeses. In reciprocation he sent back to me some Spanish wine and some cheeses! I hear that they never did eat our cheese but have kept it in their museum in Toledo"

"So, in my service for the Crown I lost my eye to the French and my arm to the Spaniards but the British Navy reigned supreme and commanded the seas and I was able to continue my career although why I remained in the Navy I cannot understand for I have always suffered from sea-sickness."

"Despite this, I had seen quite a number of other battles in my time, mainly in the Mediterranean and invariably, it seems, against France or Spain. We have also sailed the Caribbean and the Americas and have had some notable successes and benefitted from the capture of treasure. I remember that one skirmish in Jamaica brought me prize money of £400 which was extremely useful given that my wife, Fanny's massive dowry never materialised. Her uncle's plantation was not, it seems, as profitable as he had led me to believe."

"And now," I asked, "what next?"

"I am now off to the admiralty to be given my orders to return to the Mediterranean for it appears that the French and the Spanish have joined forces to invade Britain and we must engage them, preferably in the Mediterranean as they come out of Cádiz. I am to command 111 ships and we shall see what lies ahead, victory, I trust. But whatever happens now I thank God that I have done my duty."

"Before I leave for sea I must go and see my *paramour* Emma and my daughter, Horatia."

As we drove up Whitehall and turned left into The Mall I saw my distinguished passenger strain his neck to look up at the column and attempt a salute with his left hand.   I thought that I saw a tear in his eye.

I deposited him at the Office of the Admiralty and Marine Affairs, just opposite the Citadel, he paid his fare and said, "Goodbye driver and thank you for listening to me."

noslenoitaroh

Guess Who Was in My Cab Today

50

Any cab driver will, I am sure, tell you that it is not at all uncommon for a passenger to unload some of their most intimate worries or concerns to you during the course of a journey. Whether it is because you have a friendly face or just that, as somebody that they will probably never ever meet again, they can feel secure in sharing some secrets without any danger of possible later embarrassment if they were to confide in someone closer.

Such was the case with a fare that I picked up in Tufton Street, Westminster from the premises of the Council for Christians and Jews. This strange figure of a man had come running out of the rather nondescript building in a manner that automatically aroused suspicion. He was dressed in a long black flowing cloak with a shawl around his upper body. The darkness of his garb seemed to accentuate his long reddish hair that merged into an equally long straggly red beard. Over one shoulder I could see a coil of rope and he was grasping a cloth bag almost in frenzy. His eyes were darting from side to side and his face twitched in, what I thought, was anger and frustration.

He almost fell into the cab and breathlessly asked to be taken to Tyburn Way at Marble Arch close to Hyde Park. As I moved off towards Victoria Street I couldn't help but watch him in my rear-view mirror. Something had clearly agitated him to such an extent that he was muttering to himself and with a mind that seemed in utter turmoil.

My first thoughts were that I should try and bring him back to the current world of rational normality. I was worried about his mental state and any implications that his behaviour might have for me.

I asked, "You don't seem to happy with life at the moment"

"No I'm not." He said, "I am in a very awkward place with some people that I thought were friends and now they have turned against me and all because I did what I thought was right." I was pleased to see that he was calming down and becoming less agitated.

He went on, "You see, I am part of a group called together by our leader to champion a better way of life away from the tyranny and over-bearing manner in which we were being treated. Our leader, we called him 'Master', chose me, along with eleven other friends, to try and change our world. I was asked to look after the money that we collected to pay for accommodation and arrange meals when necessary but after a while things started to go wrong and I was dissatisfied with the line that the Master was taking."

"Let me give you an example," he continued, "I found that some new members were spending money on silly things like oils and body cosmetics, money that we could make better use of to help others. I remonstrated about this but nobody listened."

"I then found that within our 'cult' there were two brothers who were trying to push themselves forward as favourites with the Master, claiming that they should always sit either side of him at meals. Even their mother took to appealing to the Master to treat them more favourably that the rest of us. She was arguing that her sons, James and John, should be treated better than others because they were among the first to be called and had been with him a long time but I was also one of the first so why them?"

"Later, I found that the 'Master' was welcoming into our group some persons who I thought unworthy and had questionable reputations that would give us a bad name if it continued. But nobody would listen to my concerns; they just kept telling me not to worry and to look after the money. I wanted to swing things back again to how we were at the beginning."

"The final straw came when, at a Passover dinner, the Master all but called me a traitor in front of the others. It was then that I decided that I must do something. I resolved to tell the authorities what was going on; I suppose that I became what we now call a 'whistle blower' but it was all for the purpose of bringing us back to our original ideals. I agreed to help these authorities monitor the group's movements and tell them when and where they might best find the Master without too much opposition. They said that they wanted to pay me for my expenses and gave me this bag of money, (he raised the cloth bag that he had been clutching) but I don't want it. It is cursed"

With that he threw the bag of money out of the window of the cab. It hit a 30 mph sign and burst on to the pavement spilling out lots of silver coins.

"It has now gone all wrong and I don't know what to do next. The others in our group don't want anything to do with me and the authorities have made it clear that they no longer have a use for me - I have served their purpose. The Master is going on trial and they will certainly convict him because of what I have told them. I have nowhere to turn." He started to sob uncontrollably and pull at his hair and his robes.

As he paid his fare he tearfully said to me, "Tell Mathias. Tell Mathias". With that he ran off into Hyde Park dragging the rope along behind him.

This encounter, more than any other in my time as a London cab driver, was the saddest that I had ever experienced.

toiracsisaduj